It's About the
Journey

It's About the
Journey

Jeffrey Petzke

IT'S ABOUT THE JOURNEY

iUniverse books may be ordered through booksellers or by contacting:

iUniverse
1663 Liberty Drive
Bloomington, IN 47403
www.iuniverse.com
844-349-9409

*Because of the dynamic nature of the Internet, any web addresses or
links contained in this book may have changed since publication and
may no longer be valid. The views expressed in this work are solely those
of the author and do not necessarily reflect the views of the publisher,
and the publisher hereby disclaims any responsibility for them.*

*Any people depicted in stock imagery provided by Getty Images are
models, and such images are being used for illustrative purposes only.
Certain stock imagery © Getty Images.*

ISBN: 978-1-6632-4926-5 (sc)
ISBN: 978-1-6632-4925-8 (e)

Library of Congress Control Number: 2022923543

Print information available on the last page.

iUniverse rev. date: 01/31/2023

Know that closure is only an idea. You may always wonder and dream about special events and people all your life. Deep in you, your soul allows contradictory feelings. Don't let them take over your life. "Work to achieve a gentle, clear ending." If you want a happy ending, you need to know where to stop the story!

Chapter 1

I never thought I would end up joining a club like Parents Without Partners, much less dragging my kids with me to the first meeting, but there we were on Saturday, November 4, 1989, standing in line at a Burger King in Bellevue, Washington, along with twenty-five other single parents and their kids. I felt just like I did when I showed up at my first high school dance without a date, but it helped to pretend that Gabe, age four, Jason, age three, and I were having an ordinary Saturday at Burger King as we had done hundreds of times before. The plan was to have lunch with club members, followed by a Saturday afternoon matinee.

"I'm done, Dad," Gabe said, swallowing his last french fry and rubbing his salty, greasy hand on his jeans. While we waited for Jason to finish his meal, I listened to bits and pieces of conversation. The dating game was in full swing.

This was not my kind of scene. I wanted to go home. I never should have let my best friend, Abbey, talk me into signing up for this. I stood up to leave, but Gabe and Jason begged me to stay so they could play with two young boys who had migrated to our table. Reluctantly, I decided to stay.

"If you don't eat your lunch, you're not going to see the movie," said a deep, raspy female voice behind me. She sounded confident as she disciplined her child. I resisted the urge to turn around, as it would have been impolite.

After lunch, we walked to the adjacent community park to let the kids play until movie time. Gabe and Jason wanted to swing.

"Push me high, Daddy!" Jason said. Gabe chimed in with his brother.

A little black girl about Jason's size stood at the swing next to him. She wore a faded pink T-shirt and a tattered pink jacket. Her afro made her round, dimpled face seem smaller than it really was. Her dark-brown baby-doll eyes slowly looked up at me.

"Dad, I think she wants to swing," Jason said.

"Want to swing?" I asked.

She smiled, deepening her dimples, and said, "Mm-hmm."

I looked for her parent but saw no other African American people in the park. What I did see was an attractive white woman who appeared to be in her early thirties, sitting at a bench forty feet away, taking a deep drag on a cigarette. Her long, dark hair fell over her shoulders as she leaned over and tapped her cigarette ashes onto the sidewalk. The sun broke briefly through the gray clouds, its rays landing on her bent-over body, radiating a red halo over her hair.

My body was interested, but my mind was not. I was not a smoker, and I never dated women who smoked. It was not a rule I was willing to break. She was a beauty though. Her legs were long and slender, and she had a nearly perfect figure. I imagined I could almost wrap my hands all the way around her waist.

She looked up and saw me staring at her. She stood up quickly and moved briskly toward me. She was about five feet ten and wore a blue silk baseball jacket, the kind you might find at a sporting goods store. Underneath was a red T-shirt tucked into faded jeans that fit her curve for curve as if it were her own skin.

I looked away and hoped I had not offended her. When I turned to help the little black girl into the swing, the woman rushed toward me. Her freckled face was clean and wholesome looking. I stepped aside to prevent her from running into me.

"Push me, will you please, sir?" the little girl asked.

The woman stepped back in silent consent. I lifted the girl into her swing and pushed her gently. She pumped her legs, swinging back and forth as fast as she could to catch up with Gabe and Jason. I pushed her again, a little harder this time, and she squealed when she caught up with the boys.

As the time inched closer to the start of the movie, the woman lifted the little girl from her swing.

"Thank you for swinging me, sir," she said, dimpling her cheeks again. Her manner of speech was surprisingly adult. She gazed at me. "You have pretty blue eyes, sir," she said.

"Thank you," I replied.

The woman stiffened, grabbed the girl's hand, and they hurried away.

We walked to the theater and sat with the rest of the group. I sat in the aisle seat and waited for the movie *Look Who's Talking*, starring John Travolta and Kirstie Alley, to start.

"Excuse me, do you mind if we sit with you?" asked the raspy female voice from lunch.

"Okay, sure," I replied, not looking up.

"If you don't mind," she said, "I would prefer sitting in the aisle seat."

With the remark, I looked up and recognized that the raspy voice belonged to the dark-haired woman from the park, the one with the curvy figure. The little girl I helped swing was standing next to her, still holding her hand.

Just to be polite, I moved down two seats. The girl sat next to me. Halfway through the movie, she surprised me by crawling into my lap. The woman glanced at me, concerned.

"I'm not going anywhere," I said.

She seemed relieved and turned back to the movie. The girl relaxed in my lap and fell into a heavy sleep. After the movie ended, with a little nudge from me, the girl woke up, and the woman carried her out of the theater. The boys and I walked to the parking lot at Burger King.

"Hello," the woman said. She and the black girl stood next to a green Hyundai parked a few spaces away from us. "I'm Cassie Baker, and this is my daughter Kyra," the woman said. "Thanks for swinging her."

Still sleepy-eyed from her nap, the girl waved feebly. Jason said hello, and Gabe waved without looking up.

"Going to pizza on Thursday?" she asked.

"I don't have my kids that night," I informed her.

"Don't you like pizza anyway?"

"I guess," I said. "Well, see you later."

I disliked pushy women and left before she said anything else. I dropped the boys off at my ex-wife's house and drove home to my new bachelor pad.

Chapter 2

After Jennifer and I divorced, my possessions included a suitcase full of clothes, a 1989 Mazda pickup truck, a black 1988 BMW 528 with a sunroof, a boat, and a pet parakeet named CK—a get-well gift from my friend Lori. She heard I was having back surgery, so she gave me the bird for entertainment during the long, bedridden days following the operation. At the pet store, Lori knew CK was the one when she stuck her hand in a birdcage full of parakeets, and CK came over and jumped on her finger right away.

CK liked to climb under my covers, hop out again, and walk away. He was smart for a bird. He went back to his cage to poop, to sleep, and to eat, though he liked to share Popsicles with me in my bed. I taught him to let me push his head down, and then he would bend way over, stand up, and walk off. He was hilarious and was good company for me after the surgery. However, CK hated noisy kids. They chased him around the room, which made him nervous. I learned to keep him in his cage when Gabe and Jason visited.

During the separation from Jen, I lived in a small apartment until the divorce became final. In the meantime, I heard about a fire-damaged condominium on Lake Sammamish at the Villa Marina, east of Seattle, where it was possible to moor the boat. The damage turned out to be a gaping twenty-eight-foot hole in the ceiling. I saw clear through to the upstairs neighbor's floor. The owners wanted to sell the place as is. I bought it for $28,000.

Abbey Bishop was in charge of remodeling my condominium while I continued to work long hours in an effort to repair my postdivorce financial situation and maintain child support payments.

Abbey was one of those people you meet once in a lifetime. We met three years earlier at a happy hour. A group of coworkers and I were having a couple of drinks after work. Abbey, her sister Meredith, and a friend were sitting at the table next to us. She was cute and a lot of fun. In the years that followed after we met, she was my mother, my companion, and my best friend.

When my marriage began to fail, I became a comfortable hermit. Going out alone was not my idea of a good time. When available, Abbey accompanied me. She propped me up in the months after the divorce. Abbey was the wife I never had. She was also married.

When Abbey volunteered to decorate my condominium, I gave her carte blanche, without hesitation. She never asked me about my taste in domestic décor, but when she was done, it was exactly what I had visualized. She decorated with a lot of black and white, including a new black leather easy chair, black entertainment center, and black bookcases. The coffee table and dining room table were black and brass with smoked-glass tops. The walls were bright white. The pictures on the walls were abstract splashes of color framed in black marble and a framed print of a bright-yellow BMW racecar, an obsession of mine at the time.

According to Abbey, a bachelor pad required a token ficus tree. Her spot for the tree was in a corner of the living room. Long brass containers crammed with hanging ivy sat on top of the bookcases. My bedroom and the second bedroom followed the same black-and-white theme, with a touch of green and burgundy here and there.

My new place was perfect for building a new life for myself. It was modern and trendy, everything I was not, but the new digs gave me a jump-start in my role as the presumed happy-go-lucky bachelor.

After I moved in, Abbey continued to take care of me, despite my protests. She stopped by once a week to clean. She made sure healthy food was in the refrigerator and pantry. If she saw signs of fast food in the trash, she left a note scolding me for not eating healthier food. In my defense, I did eat bags full of "green popcorn," my term for frozen peas, straight from the freezer. I knew how to make a great Top Ramen salad with grapes and green onions tossed in and some sesame oil for taste. I tried once to cook a potato in the microwave, but it exploded. Abbey told me later that you poke holes in it with a knife before microwaving.

I hounded Abbey to accept payment for all she was doing to help me, but she refused. I sneaked money into her car ashtray, and when Abbey's husband, Matt, a contractor, experienced a downturn in business, Abbey accepted my invitation for them to use my checkbook to keep them afloat until business picked up. When their kids, Doug and Stacey, dropped in for a visit, I left money in Doug's backpack and made sure Stacey had some spending money.

Abbey made my transition from married and not interested to single and available much less painful. I worried though that Matt objected to his wife taking time away from him and the kids to care for me. I would have objected if Abbey were my wife.

Chapter 3

Matt Bishop was a tall, gentle man, a reliable husband and good father, but he worked long hours and had little time to spend with Abbey and the kids. Matt was the tail that steadied Abbey's kite, but I was her soaring partner. If Matt objected when Abbey finally told him about me, I never knew about it. When she invited me to their home for the first time, I was surprised when Matt graciously welcomed me at the front door. The Bishop family took me in, no questions asked. Soon I was Doug and Stacey's Uncle Jeff.

Most families have a thorn-in-the-side member, and in the Bishop family it was Abbey's mother, Dorothy. She was a cold, strident woman who had a habit of blurting out whatever was on her mind. Although Abbey loved and felt close to her mother, at times Dorothy frustrated her too.

A few months after Abbey and I met, Abbey's mother asked her, "Are you and Jeff interested in each other?"

"We're friends, you know, buddies, Mom," Abbey told her.

"Pals may be friends, but buddies sleep together," replied Dorothy, raising her eyebrows at her daughter.

"Mom, that's enough!" Abbey shouted.

Matt and Abbey were cold to Dorothy for a while after that. In my opinion, Dorothy was a pain in the ass. Neither Abbey nor I knew when we first met that Dorothy was also my biological father's sister. Thus, incredibly, Abbey was my first cousin. Later on, I called Abbey's mom my Auntie Sis.

To understand my relationship with Abbey, you had to be there on the night we first met. Things were different between Abbey and Matt then. Their marriage had hit a rough spot, and according to Abbey, they had officially separated but were living together because they could not afford to live apart. When the tense atmosphere at home overwhelmed her, Abbey, her sister, and a friend would hang out at Saratoga's Trunk, a popular nightclub in Bellevue at the time. She was angry and hurt, and as an act of rebellion, she took her wedding ring off and went looking for a good time, dancing and having fun. I was separated from Jen at the time and angry too, as well as lonely and vulnerable.

Saratoga's Trunk was a favorite nightclub of mine. The atmosphere was upbeat. The tables were real tree trunks. It was fun to dine in a Pepsi bottle or in an old Cadillac or Ford Thunderbird from the 1950s. The salad bar was a hollowed-out 1950 MG.

Abbey was a petite, redheaded doll, full of energy. I noticed her right away. She and her two companions approached our table and asked us to dance. I was a lousy dancer, but she was cute, and I had enough liquor in me not to care, so I said sure. Her positive mood lifted my spirits.

After a dance or two, they joined us at our table. She and the girls drank wine, and I drank Bailey's Irish Cream, my usual. It had been years since I allowed myself to be carefree. It felt innocent and slightly naughty.

I went back to Saratoga's Trunk several times after that. Abbey and I ran into each other often, and we became friends. It was easy being with her. I felt as if I had always known her. Our conversations were playful and flirty, but we never crossed the line, though I thought about it a lot. We talked about everything and eventually shared our childhood memories and family histories. After comparing notes, we put two and two together and were shocked to discover that we were cousins.

At first, it took the fun out of being with Abbey. I thought I had finally met "the one" and felt weird about the whole thing. We both did. It was awkward for a while, but we stuck it out and settled into a pair of comfortable close cousins, just not the kissing kind. That was for Jerry Lee Lewis and his kinfolk down south.

Three years after Abbey and I met, her marriage to Matt was solid and happy again, and she was still my best friend. Gabe and Jason had new cousins to play with, and I was happy to be Stacey and Doug's doting Uncle Jeff.

Chapter 4

On the way home from dropping off the boys at Jen's, after that first Parents Without Partners meeting, I thought about whether I should continue attending the group socials. Gabe and Jason had a good time, but I was ambivalent. Later that night, as I was getting ready for bed, the phone rang.

"Want to go to church with us tomorrow?" Abbey asked. It was her routine Saturday night phone call about church, but this time she was more interested in knowing what had happened at the meeting. She listened while I told her play-by-play about the dark-haired woman and the little black girl. Abbey was in my face when she wanted to give me advice about matters of the heart, whether I asked for it or not.

"Go to the pizza party Thursday," she said.

"I don't see the point, Abbey. I don't have the kids with me then."

"You have to go."

"She's not my kind of woman. I don't go out with every woman I'm attracted to."

"Do I have to call Jen and ask permission for you to pick up the boys on Thursday?"

"Don't be silly, Abbey."

"This woman is interested in you, Jeff. You don't have to marry her, you know. You need to get out more. Go and have some fun."

Since learning that we were first cousins, Abbey's new pet project was my love life—or lack thereof.

"Okay, I'll go, but she's not my type."

"Good," she said pleasantly.

The kind of woman I wanted had everything to do with my upbringing. I was born somewhere in Washington State, and even though I attempted to discover the details of my birthplace, I never found out. Hazel and Boyd Pulaski adopted me when I was young. They raised me along with their biological son and daughter. My adoptive parents were strict conservatives who believed in hard work, traditional values, and raising their kids with the backs of their hands and a good Bible lesson. We went to church every week at the Christian Science church on Mercer Island. It was the only Christian Science church in the Seattle area in those days. I upheld the values and doctrines of the church until Grandma Marie died. I was seventeen at the time.

Grandma Marie was Hazel's mother. She loved me and protected me as if she were my own mother. Hazel and I had problems as far back as I could remember, but Grandma Marie was always there to protect me from Hazel's fury. I never understood what Hazel was trying to beat out of me, but she kept at it until I was too big to strap. It was no secret that she preferred her biological children and considered me an outsider.

Hazel was a legend in her own mind. She had many colorful friends who loved to listen to her verbal yarns, and she indeed was a gifted storyteller. Hazel thought she knew everything about everyone and kept her friends mesmerized with legends of our town's settlers. I never knew if her stories were true, but I suspected that she embellished them to keep the crowd interested. What mattered most to Hazel was being the center of attention, not only within her family but also in the community.

In high school, I participated in ROTC and in student government. My best friend since grade school, Clint Harris, and I did everything together. We camped, hunted, and fished in the Cascade Mountains. We water-skied in the summer and snow-skied in the winter. Every day after school, we spent hours working on all kinds of automobile engines, a mutual passion of ours.

Life in rural Washington was good. We had rough times, sure, but being with Clint made me forget the bad.

I graduated from high school in 1974, the same year President Nixon resigned and the Vietnam War began to wind down. It was a year of rising gas prices and waiting in long lines at the pump. CRT displays and word-processing machines had rapidly replaced the old IBM Selectric typewriters. The headline news was all about Patty Hearst's kidnapping, the bank robbery, and the trial.

I was anxious to begin my life away from Hazel, but before I set out in the world to accomplish dreams and aspirations, I needed answers that only my biological parents could provide.

Chapter 5

Like most adopted kids, I dreamed of meeting my real parents. I spent the summer of 1974 diligently looking for them, and my efforts paid off. I found and met my real father. We had lunch at a deli near the Pike Place Market in downtown Seattle. He spotted me right away.

"You look like your mother," he said, motioning me to sit down.

He was an obese, ruddy-nosed, unkempt, bleary-eyed old man. I had his blue eyes but saw no further resemblance to myself in him. He looked and smelled as if he had not bathed in a while.

My father took over two hours telling me his story. His conversation was scattered and confusing. It was difficult for me to decipher a simple timeline of events in his life. He was easily distracted and would lose his train of thought and go off on a tangent. My attempts to steer him back on course failed.

Later, at his home, I studied notes and tried to make sense out of what he told me. If what he said was accurate, which I doubted, he had been married seven times. He told me that my real mother passed away years ago. I also learned that I had a half-sister, but my father had no idea where she was. He saw her only once before giving her up. My half-sister and I at least had that in common. During our visit, he never asked about my life, which in retrospect, seemed fitting.

After our visit, I never saw or heard from my father again, which was fine with me. I came away with two new truths about myself: I inherited rotten to the core genes, and I was proud of my status as an orphan. Other than that, the rest of my family history remained unknown. That summer, I made a vow to my unborn offspring that I would do everything in my power to be the kind of father I never had.

My adoptive family believed in the military, so I did what an obedient and grateful adopted son would do: I joined the military in the fall of 1974 and spent the next eight years of my life serving my country, learning the rules of order, following them, and making sure everyone else did too. Military life gave me the structure I needed. I learned the importance of a well-planned life. I participated in several important efforts that I believe laid the foundation, good or bad, for who I am today.

During my military career, my stations were in Vietnam, Alaska, Kansas, Panama, Iran, the Congo, and Korea. Fort Riley, Kansas, was a Midwestern hellhole, but I liked the nice little house I lived in, where buffalo would graze at my back fence.

In 1978, while still in the military, I met Jennifer Sanchez at a Halloween party. She was a sexy, exotic beauty. I fell in love with her hard and fast. In the past, women had pursued me, but this time I was the one who pursued Jen. We married immediately, and in the beginning, we were happy.

I finished my electrical engineering degree while in the military in New York, at the Rochester Institute of Technology.

When my duty in the military ended, I went back to Washington State. Engineering jobs were scarce in my hometown, so I asked around and got a job working in a Goodyear tire store. Then I worked construction, but they laid me off.

In 1982, I talked to Senator Henry "Scoop" Jackson, who sent me to the director of the Employment Securities, after which I got a job with the Washington State Patrol. My experience in the military helped me land the job. It was a steady income with fair pay.

After a while, though, I began to realize that my years working in the military, along with my job with the state patrol had taken a toll on my family. I thought I could straighten out the lives around me by enforcing the rules. I believed in living life by the book and thought everyone else should too. It looked good on paper but not in real life with real people.

Toward the end of my tenure with the state patrol, I confronted Jerry, Hazel's biological son and my adoptive brother, about his drug and alcohol use, but my intervention ended the relationship.

In 1985, Gabe was born with his mother's olive skin and a full head of dark hair. Eleven months after that, Jason was placed in my arms, fair-skinned, blue-eyed, and blond like me.

It was during this time that Jen and I began having serious marital problems. Her drug use had increased over the years, to the point that I refused to put up with it anymore, children or no children. It was time to take action. I left work early one afternoon, went home, and confronted her.

"Drugs or me," I said.

"Drugs," she replied.

Our marriage became an "in name only" marriage after that.

I was sick of playing good with everyone around me, so I quit. Soon after, I created a start-up company called Mobile Marine. I repaired boat radios on location. Boat owners no longer had to haul their boats to an install shop on the other side of town. This proved to be a successful niche in the market, and within the first year, Mobile Marine was profitable.

Our marital problems continued to spiral out of control as the months passed, but when I thought about leaving, I thought it would be in the boys' best interest to wait until they were a little older.

Jen ultimately made the decision to end the marriage for me. She walked into the house after staying out all night, plopped her purse down on the kitchen table, looked at me eye to eye, and said, "I want a divorce."

There was nothing left to say after that, but our lawyers had discussions, plenty of them. We went to court thirty-six times from 1986 to 1988, embroiled in a bitter custody battle. As part of the divorce settlement, I had to sell Mobile Marine and give half of the proceeds to Jen.

Abbey's entrance into my life after Jen and I separated mercifully tempered my three-year war with Jen. After a brutal round in court, I would collapse in a corner while Abbey wiped my brow with a fresh towel and pep-talked me until I was ready to go at it again.

After the divorce settlement, I began freelancing as an electrical engineer. I was overweight and out of shape. With Abbey's encouragement, I joined a gym and entered a period in my life that I called my "pretty boy days."

I worked out seven days a week and pushed back from the table. I lost 115 pounds and was tanned, muscle-bound, and strong at 185 pounds. I shaved my bushy red beard and bought some new clothes. Lifting weights became an addiction, which added to the many back surgeries I had since a major injury in the army. I bought a 1987 red Triumph Spitfire, my dream car at the time. After I had acquired all the trappings of a happy bachelor, I was ready to get on with my life again.

The quest for my ideal woman began again. I was an easy mark for smart, sexy women with shiny, sparkly red hair; a trim but curvy body; polished nails; and spike heels. She had to come from a good family who treated her lovingly and groomed her to uphold traditional values. Laughing at my jokes was a plus.

Historically, I dated women who appeared initially to have decent morals, but I broke it off when I heard about them drinking or taking drugs. I would need to observe my ideal woman with Gabe and Jason. If she fit all my prerequisites but failed to connect with my boys, I would back off.

This time I would stick to my plan and force myself to remain objective for as long as possible. The task ahead would not be easy for me, because I was a natural-born romantic, a real sap when I fell in love. I knew I would have to be smart this time. I was determined to learn from my mistakes with Jen.

The woman from the park was another mistake, no doubt about it. Besides, the black daughter was a deal-breaker in and of itself. Everyone I knew in our small town was racist, including me. We laughed at racial jokes about as much as we laughed at dumb blonde jokes. It was harmless fun to us. Of course, we would never be so rude as to tell a dumb blonde joke in front of a real-live blonde-haired girl. It was easier still to dot our conversations with racial slurs, since no black people lived in our town, thus no fear of reprisals.

We were not bad white people, not at all. We listened to the echoes of our ancestors, whom the Bible taught us to respect and obey.

Loyalty mattered to us and to me especially—even in the face of evidence that it may be undeserved. Grandma Marie drilled into me at an early age that an honorable man was a loyal man, first to God, then family, community, and country. My time in the military further entrenched my belief in the virtues of loyalty.

It would take some kind of act of God to pry me away from my beliefs. I was not entirely sure I would recognize it even if God designed one with my name on it.

Chapter 6

On November 9, 1989, while the rest of the world watched the Berlin Wall come down on television, the boys and I were at Pietro's Pizza at our second Parents Without Partners meeting, munching on pepperoni pizza. The same crowd was there, except for the woman from the park. Afterward, I cleaned up our table while the boys played with their new friends. As we were about to leave, the woman from the park pulled into the parking lot. Her black daughter with the dimpled smile was in the car with her.

"I went to the wrong pizza parlor," she said as she passed by us.

Again, she wore no makeup, and her hair was damp. She was dressed in the same blue jeans, T-shirt, and blue silk baseball jacket.

There she is, the big mistake with a great body. The boys and I left.

A week later, we were at another Parents Without Partners meeting, this time at Chuck E. Cheese.

"This is for me being late last time," said the woman from the park, holding a pitcher of beer in one hand and the black girl's hand with the other. "Well? Do we get to sit down?" she said.

Abbey was right. The woman was obviously in hot pursuit, but all I could think about was her daughter. Where was her black daddy anyway? The possibility disgusted me.

Where are my manners? It is none of my business who the father is.

"Sure, have a seat," I said.

We chatted over beer and pizza. I gave the boys money to get tokens, and they hurried away to their favorite arcade games.

"Mommy, can I go with them?" the girl asked, searching her mother's face.

The woman looked to me for approval, but I was not happy with the idea of the boys playing with her.

"Please, sir, may I?" the little girl asked, her dark eyes glistening earnestly at me.

"Okay," I replied.

She thanked me and ran to catch up with the boys.

Chuck E. Cheese was the new hot venue for families. Kids could roam freely without their parents close by. The air smelled of a foul mixture of Hawaiian Punch, pizza sauce, and dirty diapers, but I learned to tolerate the smell because it was cheaper than hiring a babysitter. The kids had fun, and the adults had time to themselves.

I was almost done with my second glass of beer when the representative in charge of the Parents Without Partners meeting approached our table. "Cassie! Jeff!" she said, shaking her head. "No drinking beer in front of the children! It's not allowed. You both know that."

I apologized. Cassie and I looked at each other, both of us trying hard not to smile. The representative went over all the rules again. Cassie apologized and thanked her for reminding us. Partners in crime, we grinned at each other after the woman left. If felt good to feel slightly naughty.

Cassie's dazzling smile and freckled face gave her a sense of wholesomeness that caught me off guard. The kids played for an hour while Cassie and I kept the conversation light and fun. At one point, we glanced around the room at the other parents and took turns pointing out the pickups in progress. I had a great time. Maybe Abbey was right about having a night of harmless fun.

Cassie cupped her hands around her mouth and called for Kyra. When she turned back toward me, our eyes locked. Something inside me uncorked. All kinds of alarms went off in my head. I looked away. I excused myself and found the boys. We walked Cassie and Kyra to Cassie's Hyundai, parked next to my truck.

On an impulse, I said, "Hey, Cassie, I have a business dinner tomorrow night. Everyone will have their spouses or girlfriends with them. I hate going to these affairs alone. Will you go with me?"

No harm, no foul, just fun, I told myself. It was the first of many self-deceptions I would be guilty of in the immediate future.

"I don't know if I can get a babysitter, but if I can, I'll meet you there," she said.

The next night, I showed up early at The Butcher restaurant, where we routinely had our business dinners. After serving appetizers, the head waiter told me that a woman had arrived and was asking for me. I excused myself and followed him to the front entrance.

Cassie stood inside the door. This time she was wearing dark-red lipstick and makeup. Her long nails were polished bright red, and she wore high heels and a long dress.

"You look nice," I said. *Hot* is what I was thinking.

"Thank you," she said nervously.

Heads turned as I led Cassie to our table. She was the prettiest woman in the room.

It was a typical throw-the-cow-on-the-table business dinner, which Cassie sat through quietly. After dinner, in the table conversation, she leaned over and whispered in my ear, "I would have called to tell you that I was running late, but I didn't have your number."

"I can fix that," I said.

I wrote my home address and my phone number on a napkin and handed it to her. She asked to borrow my pen, scribbled her number, and gave it to me.

After dinner, the men talked business. Cassie joined the women who had gathered in a group apart from the men. The more I caught myself turning in Cassie's direction to stare at her, the more my stomach reminded me that I was wading into troubled waters. It was a relief when Cassie stepped away from the group and signaled me. She pointed to her watch. I excused myself and joined her.

"I'm sorry, Jeff. Babysitter issues," she said.

I walked her to her car and offered to pay the babysitter. She declined. She lifted her face, her brown eyes staring deeply into mine, and lingered just long enough to sound the alarm in my stomach again. Swiftly she kissed my cheek and then hopped into her car and drove away. Her spontaneity amused and aroused me. The cool night air touched the wet place on my cheek.

"Hey, Jeff, did your date have a good time?" the wife of one of my coworkers said as she passed by on the way to the restroom.

"I don't know. Ask her," I said. "Oh, and by the way, it was not an official date."

"The lipstick on your cheek says it was," she said, giggling and winking as she looked back at me.

Chapter 7

I grew up in the sixties at Grandma Marie's knee. What I did not learn from Grandma, Hazel beat into me. I thought of both of them as I drove home.

What am I doing? This woman has a black kid! Grandma taught me better.

A week and a half later, I pushed back in my easy chair and watched the Seahawks play the Giants at Giants' Stadium. A loyal Seahawks fan since 1976, I never missed a home game. Quarterback Kelly Stouffer was having a bad day, and the Hawks were in the middle of another losing season. The score was Giants 15, Seattle 3.

The phone rang, but I was not about to let the outside world interfere during game time. The caller did not leave a message. Unfortunately, it kept ringing on and off until I finally answered during a commercial break.

"Do you have time for drinks on Monday?" Cassie asked.

"Sorry, I'm leaving town on business," I lied. I was in no mood to deal with the racial thing with Cassie, and I was not sure I trusted myself to be with her without giving in to the attraction again. I went back to the game, relieved that the phone call was short and over.

Later that evening, Abbey called. "What's the news? Catch me up."

"Nothing, and I like it that way," I replied. But Abbey continued to pry until I told her about the call from Cassie.

"I have decided not to see her again," I informed her.

"Why?"

"Her daughter is black, Abbey. It's too much for me to deal with. It's as simple as that."

"Why don't you ask her for a real date?" Abbey asked.

"You are officially out of your mind, woman. You heard what I just said, right?"

"Yes, but think about it, will you?"

"I already have."

"You had fun with her, didn't you?"

"That's not the point."

"It most certainly is. Tell you what, I can fix you up with a blind date, or you can take out a woman you have had fun with already. It's your choice."

"I choose none of the above."

After living with Hazel for eighteen years, my tendency was to avoid bullheaded women instead of locking horns with them. But Abbey was cute, and it was fun to spar with her.

"Okay, I'll think about it."

The next morning, Abbey called again. "Have you called Cassie yet?"

"No."

"Well, when are you?"

"You're such a pest."

"You will call her tomorrow?"

"I don't know, maybe."

The next day, she called again, this time at the office. I told my secretary to tell her I was away from my desk. After work, I went up to the gym, and when I got home, the light on the answering machine was blinking.

"You can run, but you can't hide," Abbey said and hung up.

I laughed and gave in. I hated disappointing her and called back.

"Why don't *you* date Cassie?" I asked.

"What's the matter, don't you have the money? I'll loan you five bucks," she bantered back.

"I knew it would come to this. Okay, you win. I'll call her tomorrow," I said.

The next day, I called Cassie. She seemed delighted to hear from me. I asked her out to dinner with me on Friday.

"I'd love to, but I don't have a babysitter. My parents usually sit for me, but they are out of town. If I can find a sitter, I'll let you know," she said.

The next morning, Cassie called. She told me she had found a sitter and that she would meet me at the restaurant. I chose the Kayak Club on Lake Union for dinner. I ate there often and felt relaxed in familiar surroundings. Wooden canoes and kayaks covered the walls, with views of Lake Union on three sides of the restaurant. My plan was to have a polite and pleasant evening, and then we would part ways. The reservation was at eight. Before I left for the restaurant, I called Abbey.

"Cassie and I are going out tonight. I didn't call sooner because I wanted to make you wait."

"I'm crushed," replied Abbey.

"Apparently, not enough to leave me alone about this."

"Relax, Jeff. Have a good time and call me as soon as you get back," she said.

Cassie was in her work clothes, gray slacks and a white button-down blouse. Her mood was businesslike. She talked about her job as a Girl Friday at a company in Bellevue that printed shiny sales catalogs for mail-order magazines. She had been working there for two years.

Her aloof manner threw me off balance. When I attempted to divert the conversation from business to personal, she resisted, staying on safe, impersonal subjects. She declined dessert and said she had to leave early because she had to work over the weekend. Our first date was over before it began.

I drove the long way home. I thought I would feel relieved that it was over. Instead, I felt confused and gloomy. Thoughts of Cassie nagged at me. It was as if she had been on the tip of my tongue but never fully articulated.

Early the next morning, Abbey called. "Did you get home okay? How was your date?"

"You're up early for a woman who likes to sleep in," I teased.

"I am indeed, and it's your fault. Now tell me everything."

We discussed the night before in detail, despite my preference to summarize. Again, I told Abbey I would not be seeing Cassie again.

"If you aren't asking her out again, why are you down about it? I can hear it in your voice."

"I honestly don't know. I have a bad feeling about this. She's hiding something, I'm sure of it."

"You don't know that, Jeff. Maybe she was just nervous."

"Maybe, but she volunteered little information about herself, despite prompts from me. It was bizarre."

"Like I said before, Jeff, you don't need to know her entire life story to hang out and have fun."

"Two words, Abbey. Remember them this time: Black. Daughter."

"That's none of your business."

"You're kidding, right? You and I both know that Hazel would chain me to a tree if she heard about it."

"Since when do you care what Hazel thinks?" Abbey asked.

"It's not about Hazel; you know that. It's socially unacceptable. I like living in my hometown trouble free. Making ripples is not my style. Just let it go. It's over."

"It's only over when you stop thinking about her."

Chapter 8

I took Abbey's words to heart and concentrated on work and spending time with Gabe and Jason. It helped for a while. Life resumed, but there had been a subtle shift inside me. Maybe it was new self-awareness.

Previously I had been happy with disciplined structure of my daily routines. It led to greater productivity at work and a sense of fulfillment but nothing more. My orderly life seemed mechanical and meaningless. I was restless and became bored easily.

"I have an idea," said Abbey.

"Your ideas are scary," I joked.

"Donald Duck and Mickey Mouse are scary?"

"Okay, I'll bite," I said.

"Disney on Ice is coming to Seattle soon. Wouldn't it be great to take the boys?"

"They would like that. I took them last year, and they had a great time."

"I was thinking ..."

"Don't think," I interrupted.

"Jeff, hear me out. My idea is that you can take Cassie and Kyra along with you and the boys this year."

"Why would I do that?"

"Because it would be fun."

"Fun for whom? You? Besides, car is in the shop, and my truck will only seat three people."

"Cassie's car will hold five, right? You could go in her car, and this would be a family event."

"Yeah, a mixed family. Give up, Abbey."

"Listen to me, Jeff. I know you're not interested in Cassie, but this would be for the boys. They'd love it. You would be treating the little girl to what is most likely her first Disney show on ice."

"Well, yes. The kids would have fun, but it won't solve the fact that the child is black."

"Oh, come on. Give her a break, Jeff! She's just a little kid."

"Okay, fine. I'll try this one more time," I said reluctantly.

Over the next few days, Abbey's annoying phone calls started again.

"Did you buy the tickets yet? How many did you buy?"

Abbey wouldn't stop calling, no matter what I said to her. I stopped answering the phone. Eventually a week went by.

Monday evening, after a long, stressful day at work, I skipped the gym and went straight home. Just as I grabbed a beer and found a seat in my recliner, the phone rang.

"Now what?" I asked, assuming it was Abbey.

"Will you take me to dinner tonight?"

It was Cassie. Just hearing her voice did things to me.

"Jeff? Are you there?"

"Yes, I'm here. I'm just surprised to hear from you."

"Pleasantly, I hope," she said cheerfully.

"Let's meet at The Butcher," I suggested.

Cassie was already there when I arrived. A cloud of smoke surrounded her face. I had forgotten about her smoking habit. I sat across from her as she lit a fresh cigarette.

"Do you mind?" I asked, looking at her cigarette.

She put her lighter back into her purse and placed her cigarette in the half-filled ashtray. She ordered a glass of white wine, and I asked for my usual Baileys. Again, she measured her words carefully, and I found myself carrying the conversation for both of us. It did not take long for me to run out of things to say, and I was willing to say anything to break the monotony.

"Do you want to go to Disney on Ice?"

"I'll have to get a sitter," she said in the same unyielding monotone.

"No, no, no. I meant that the kids would go with us."

"Oh, okay. Sure, we will go." Her lack of enthusiasm convinced me that she was keeping me in the dark about something.

My growing frustration emboldened me to speak frankly. "Cassie, what's wrong?"

If she responded with "nothing," I was going to leave. She kept her eyes down as she focused on the ashtray near her. It was as if I had never asked the question. When she looked up, it was not at me.

"I'm leaving," she said as she grabbed her purse and walked out the door, leaving me alone feeling like a fool.

I had lunch with Abbey the next day. She listened to my account of what had happened.

"Do you think she's married?" Abbey asked.

"Well, remember, she is in Parents Without Partners."

Abbey's eyes widened. "You don't believe all Parents Without Partners members are single, do you?"

"That's not something I think about, but since you brought it up, no, I don't think she's married, at least not now, maybe before."

On Sunday morning, December 3, I had planned to stay home and watch football, but I was too restless to sit still. I grabbed a cup of hot coffee and my house keys and walked down to the dock to check on my boat. The National Weather Service had issued a high wind advisory for the day. A cold front was moving in from Canada. I secured the boat and watched the wind pick up until the choppy lake water formed waves large enough to wash over the dock. It began to sleet. The wind riddled me with stinging bullets of ice. I walked back to the condominium, where the phone was ringing.

"Are you mad at me or just busy?" asked Cassie. Her voice sounded bright and cheerful again.

"Neither."

"I'm sorry about walking out on you."

"If you mean that, meet me in an hour at Black Angus. I need to get a few things off my chest."

Cassie was thirty minutes late. Again, she was standoffish and silent, and this time, so was I. After what seemed an hour, she spoke. "What's on your mind?"

"Why haven't you given me your address?"

She stiffened but remained seated. "Anything else?" she asked.

"That's my question. What is it that you aren't telling me, Cassie?"

She did not answer, but I detected a flash of anger. With each drop in the temperature between us, I saw no reason not to be blunt with her.

"Why did you agree to go with me to Disney on Ice?"

"I don't know," she said defiantly.

"Cassie, are you married?"

"No, never have been," she said without hesitation.

Again, I waited for her to speak. She didn't. This time I was the one who walked out. I paid the bill and left without saying good-bye.

Chapter 9

The minute I got home, I called Abbey. "She's not married and says she's never been married."

"Poor girl. It can't be easy being a single mother. Her plate is probably big and full," Abbey said.

"I don't get it. Why are you still defending her?" I asked.

"Because we still don't know her story."

On Monday before Disney on Ice, Cassie called. "Do you want to take me to dinner tomorrow?"

"I guess we do need to firm up our plans if Disney is still on," I said half-heartedly.

"Do you have a pencil and a piece of paper?" she asked.

I grabbed a notepad, and she gave me her home address. I offered to pick her up for dinner, and she said yes. Immediately after we hung up, I drove over to the address to check it out. I did not see the house number that she gave me, so I circled the neighborhood again, this time looking down driveways. It was barely visible and behind another house. A muddy gravel driveway led to an old garage in the backyard. It was a single-car garage and was in disrepair. The roof sagged with a heavy growth of bright-green moss. Part of the doorway was duct-taped.

The next night, I drove to her place to pick her up. I knocked and waited. The smell of mold and mildew made me cough. Cassie opened the door, smiled nervously, and invited me in.

The room was small and sparse. A portable CD player sat on top of a badly scarred early American end table. Next to the table was a weather-beaten, rose-colored loveseat. Two black vinyl recliner chairs sat adjacent to the loveseat. The room was clean and in order.

"Where's Kyra?" I asked.

"She's next door playing at the neighbor's. My neighbor is babysitting for me tonight."

Cassie stepped into the bedroom to get her coat. I followed her. Twin beds pulled close together crammed the small room, and there was not much room for anything else. Her clothes hung from a makeshift rod suspended from the ceiling. I helped her with her coat.

We drove to Jungle Jim's at Bellevue Square for dinner. In the truck on the way over, Cassie gave me the silent treatment again. After the server seated us, Cassie closed her menu and looked up at me. "Do you have a problem with where I live?"

"Do *you* have a problem with where you live?"

"It's what I can afford."

"No, Cassie, I don't have a problem with it."

Having cleared the air between us, Cassie's eyes brightened, and she began to smile again. In a matter of minutes, she was charming and flirty. We ordered drinks and talked without interruption throughout the evening.

"I hate baseball," Cassie said.

"Then why do you wear a baseball jacket all the time?" I asked.

"It's just a jacket," she said, "just something I throw on when I'm not working."

We talked about the kids and about parenting in general. We shared our likes and dislikes in music, movies, TV, politics, and a number of other categories. It was a relaxed, fun night. We were outrageous flirts. The longer the evening lasted, the more I realized that despite the rules I lived by, this woman was beginning to get to me.

The restaurant and the entire mall closed at midnight. The mall security guard let us out the back entrance, and we walked around the mall parking lot deep in conversation. We were like a couple of high school kids staying out past curfew. At three in the morning, I took Cassie home and walked her to her front door.

"Do you want to come in?" she asked.

"No, it's late," I said.

As I turned to leave, Cassie kissed my mouth hard. I kissed back. She didn't break away.

My world fell away. Her mouth was all that existed. I wrapped my arms around her and pulled her into me. She was incredibly responsive. Suddenly, she pulled away from me and studied my face. She seemed pleased with what she saw. The kiss left blushed blotches around her mouth.

I ran my forefinger softly along her jawline and kissed her, lightly touching her lips. I thanked her for a great evening and waited in the truck until she was safely inside with the door locked.

I took the long way home, feeling happy. I sang along with the radio, grinning from ear to ear. I was smitten, and I wanted more.

As I approached the condominium, I began to deflate, as I thought about Kyra and the inevitable negative repercussions of living in a racially mixed family.

"Nobody wants mixed-race kids," Grandma Marie used to say.

"The only thing worse than a black family is a black-and-white family," Hazel would say.

I thought about what could happen to Gabe and Jason once word spread that they had a black stepsister. I also feared that Jen would sue for full custody if I pursued a relationship with Cassie and Kyra. The scary thing was that I was actually thinking of ways to work things out. Gabe and Jason came first. No amount of personal pleasure was worth subjecting my sons to shame and rejection. I remembered the promise I had made to the kids. When I drove into the condominium parking lot, I was exhausted from my self-imposed duel. I passed the answering machine on my way to bed. It was blinking with messages.

The first message was from Abbey. "Call me when you get this. I want to hear all about your evening."

The second was from Cassie. "Hi. Thanks again for dinner. I had a blast. Sleep well."

Hearing Cassie's voice carried me back to her front door, to her lips and the kiss.

This had to be some kind of fallout from the divorce or midlife crisis or temporary insanity. I was a crazy man wielding a hatchet, splitting myself open right down the middle. I left the condo and went down to the dock to be near the water. There would be no sleep tonight. I sat on the dock until daybreak, swaying back and forth from a guilt-ridden stupor to a keen sense of awakening for the first time in my life. A couple of hours later, I showered, drank a quick cup of coffee, and drove into work, still not the least bit sleepy.

"Good morning, Jeff. Someone left a message on your desk," my secretary Mary Jane said, smiling more than usual.

Sitting on my desk was a single rosebud in a crystal vase. In the center of the attached card was a single handwritten letter C.

Chapter 10

I called Abbey and asked her to meet me for lunch. We found a quiet place, and I filled Abbey in on the previous evening's events, including the kiss, the impact it had on me, and how I seemed unwilling or unable to get Cassie out of my mind.

"If you're a white woman and you give birth to a black child, should you be dating a white man or a black man?" I asked.

"Does it matter?"

"Yes … no. I don't know. What's your opinion?"

"My opinion isn't important."

"Maybe we should keep it light, you know, just friends. We could try that."

"Most men and women find it difficult being friends only, Jeff. Remember how it was with us before we found out we were related?"

"Yes, and thank God we never crossed the line," I said.

"Have you and Cassie, you know, done it?"

"No, no, but I think about it all the time, and it makes me crazy."

"So, you've decided to continue seeing her?"

"That depends on which part of me you're talking to."

Disney on Ice came to town on Friday, December 15. I left my truck at Cassie's place, and the five of us piled into Cassie's Hyundai. We parked and found our seats in the front row. Kyra was too excited to stay seated.

"When will it start, Mommy?"

"Soon," Cassie said.

Kyra turned to me. "Is Snow White here?"

"Yes," I said.

"And the Seven Dwarfs too, Kyra," Gabe added.

"Yippee!" Kyra shouted, clapping and jumping in place.

"Mickey Mouse too? And Goofy? What about Cinderella?" Kyra asked.

"Yes, they are all here," I said.

When the master of ceremonies skated to the center and spoke to the crowd, Kyra stopped the rapid-fire questions, sat down, and watched the show, enraptured by what she saw. After the show, we walked by a trinket stand.

"Please, Daddy, can we get something?" the boys asked.

"No," I said. They knew not to ask again.

Kyra followed suit. "Please, Mommy?"

"No," Cassie said.

"But, Mommy—please, please," she begged.

"No, honey," Cassie said.

Kyra lost it. She screamed and fell to the floor onto her back, kicking wildly.

"Calm down, honey," Cassie said, blushing. "You're embarrassing me."

She attempted to pick up Kyra and calm her down, but Kyra screamed louder and kicked harder until Cassie let go.

Gabe and Jason hid behind me. Cassie looked at me with exasperation. People passing by us began to stare. They had to be thinking the same thing I thought whenever I saw a child have a temper tantrum out in public: *What is wrong with the parents? Can't they control their own child?*

"You take the boys, Cassie. I'll meet you at the car," I told her.

After they left, I lifted Kyra up and held her in my arms. She kicked and screamed, but I was stronger than she was. I continued a steady hold on her until she stopped resisting me. I carried her to a quiet corner away from the crowd and sat her on top of a covered trashcan.

She stopped screaming. We looked at each other for a while without speaking. She rubbed her wet eyes and began hiccupping, soothing herself with soft moans.

"Kyra?" I said.

She looked up at me, her eyes swollen and irritated.

When I was sure she was listening, I said, "Your mom loves you very much and gives you what you need, but she can't always give you what you want."

Her small, tired shoulders slumped.

"Do you understand?"

She nodded while she tried to catch her breath.

I surprised myself with what I did next. I patted her back gently, leaned down, and kissed her forehead. She calmed down right away. I picked her up and put her feet down on the floor beside me. She grabbed my hand, and we walked to the car together.

"It must be the magic of a man," Cassie said as Kyra and I approached the car.

The ride home was quiet. Kyra and the boys fell into a sound sleep.

"What did you do to calm her down?" Cassie whispered.

"I'm not sure if I know," I said.

"Did you tell her you were embarrassed or upset?"

"No. That would have made matters worse."

"Amazing," Cassie replied.

At Cassie's place, I carried Gabe and Jason to my truck. Then I carried Kyra into the bedroom, tucked her into bed, and kissed her good night.

Cassie walked me to the door, and we held each other for a long time. I kissed her in the small place below her right ear. She made a soft, arousing sound. I said good night before things got out of hand.

After taking the boys back to their mom's house, I drove the long way home. Kyra somehow had slipped through the massive walls of things taboo inside me and pulled me close to her, and for a fleeting moment, I sensed a new and profound capacity for openness and flexibility toward life. The moment passed quickly, and years later, I would remember it with nostalgia.

On Sunday after church and over lunch, I told Abbey and Matt about Kyra's temper tantrum at the Disney show.

"Are you sure you want to take this on?" Matt asked.

"No, I'm not sure at all," I said.

"If you choose to commit to this woman and her child, there will be no turning back. If there's a problem, you will have to be part of the solution," he said.

Abbey nodded in agreement.

Of course, Matt was right, but coming up with a solution was not going to be easy. I pressured myself to make a decision. I needed to break up with Cassie before Christmas or decide to go ahead with it. It would be cruel for me to invite them over for the holidays if my intention was to stop seeing them.

A couple of days later, Cassie and Kyra met the boys and me at Chuck E. Cheese. After the kids left to play arcade games, Cassie and I talked about Kyra's tantrums.

"She has them all the time. I don't know how to handle her meltdowns," Cassie said. "I can tell when one is coming on. That's when I get nervous and lock myself in the bathroom until she calms down."

"Weird," I said.

"I don't know what else to do, Jeff. I'm afraid I'll do something I'll regret later," she said as she pondered and nervously rolled strands of her long hair around her forefinger.

On Friday, Cassie and I went to dinner and a movie. The movie was so bad that we walked out soon after it started. We walked to the corridors inside the mall and talked instead.

At Sears, I pulled her into an alcove with a three-way mirror and kissed her.

"Let's go to my place," she whispered.

We spent the next hour curled up on Cassie's loveseat, kissing and holding each other. The hour passed quickly. When Cassie left to pick up Kyra at the sitter's house, I drove home with the sudden realization that I had stopped thinking of Kyra as black. Kyra was simply Kyra. I wanted to protect her and love her as if she were my own flesh and blood.

There it was, the decisive moment. There would be no turning back. I would find a way to protect the boys and at the same time keep Cassie and Kyra in our lives.

Chapter 11

I found myself caught up in the spirit of Christmas, a rarity for me. I was happy to be out shopping. In the past, Christmas shopping had been a time-consuming obligation that I dreaded every year. Cassie and I stood in the back of a long line of shoppers, waiting our turn at the register, a circumstance that virtually guaranteed impatient frustration on my part. However, this year, I enjoyed whittling away the time, flirting shamelessly and holding hands with Cassie. After we finished shopping, I took Cassie home and paid the babysitter, despite Cassie's protests.

As I was leaving, Cassie said, "Tell me the truth, Jeff. How do Gabe and Jason really feel about Kyra?"

"They have never mentioned that Kyra is black, if that's what you want to know."

Cassie nodded and smiled.

"But they do have big problem with her temper," I added.

"So do I," she said quietly. "She can be a stinker, and I don't know what to do about it. I hope it's just a phase that she'll grow out of."

Later in the day, Abbey and I went for a round of shopping.

"Hey, look at you, Santa. You're going crazy buying presents this year," she said.

"I guess I did go a bit overboard."

"There's something different about you this Christmas."

"It's Cassie. I've never met anyone quite like her, and I think I want to hang around and see what happens."

"Be careful, Jeff. Try not to let your expectations of Cassie get out of hand."

"Is that what I'm doing?"

"It's just that you're going through the first blush with Cassie. Take your time, enjoy yourself, and keep in mind that reality is inevitable and could disappoint you."

As we strolled in and out of the stores, I reassured Abbey that although my head was in the clouds, I would make sure both feet stayed firmly planted on the ground. We loaded all the gifts in my truck.

"I need a tree and decorations," I said.

Abbey laughed. "Isn't it a little late to start thinking about a tree?"

"I'm serious, Abbey. I'm going to invite Cassie and Kyra over for Christmas Eve with the boys."

I had never been enthusiastic about decorating for the holiday, but this year I wanted the whole shebang.

"Tell you what: Meredith and I will see what we can come up with in the next twenty-four hours," Abbey said.

I gave her a big bear hug. "Thanks, Abbey. What would I do without you?"

"You would have Christmas without decorations," she said, winking at me. "Now get out of here. I have some decorating to do."

The phone rang for a long time before she answered it.

"Hel-lo," Cassie answered, her voice quivering. It was difficult to hear her with Kyra's screams going on in the background.

"Kyra's lost it again, huh?" I asked.

"I had to let myself out of the bathroom to answer the phone," she shouted.

"Mind if I try to cheer things up over there?" I asked loudly.

"You can try," she yelled.

"Will you and Kyra come to my place tomorrow for a Christmas Eve celebration?"

"Yes! We'd love to!" she said. "I'll call you after things have settled down here." With that, she hung up.

On Christmas Eve morning, I woke up early, excited about the evening. I dressed in a hurry and went to the office. The project I was working on was almost complete, and I wanted to wrap it up before the holidays. However, once at the office, I found it difficult to focus. Finally, in the late afternoon, I gave up and went home.

The whole place was lit up. Multicolored lights draped the bushes, the deck, the windows, and the front door. A fresh evergreen wreath was tied with a huge red velvet bow on the front door.

I unlocked the door and went in. A floor-to-ceiling evergreen tree decorated heavily with pine cones, green glass beads, feathered blue jays, robins, and miniature lights covered the tree. Large baskets filled with shiny red, yellow, and green Washington apples sat at the foot of the tree.

The smells of homemade garlic bread and lasagna led me to the kitchen. Hot apple cider was steaming in the Crock-Pot. I noticed a handwritten note on the dining table:

Have a Merry Christmas. See you tomorrow. Love, Abbey.

My cousin and her sister had done an incredible job.

I changed into a Polo shirt and slacks and drove to Jen's to get the boys. On the way, I stopped by Hazel's house to drop off some presents.

"What the hell are you thinking, son?" Hazel said with fury in her eyes.

I stepped back, an arm's length away from her. Her eyes narrowed, and she flushed bright red. "I raised you better than to hang around with white trash. Have you lost your mind? How dare you date a white woman with a black kid!" she yelled.

"Who told you?"

"You're a disgrace to this family," she said. "I know all about it. You know good and well that once a white woman sleeps with a black man, no decent white man would have her! Are you so hard up for a female that you have to stoop this low? For the love of God, son, you have gone off the deep end this time! Are you listening to me?"

"How did you find out?" I repeated calmly.

"Abbey's mother told her sister, who told Rip Doyle, who told Hank Gibson, who told me. The whole family is embarrassed to death."

"Well, I'm sorry you didn't hear it from me," I said.

"I didn't raise you as my own for you to do this to me," she said. "You know how folks treat half-breeds, son. White people don't want them; coloreds don't want them either. Mulattos are nothing but trouble," she barked. "Everyone knows they're just uppity nig—"

"Okay, stop now," I interrupted.

"Did you forget? You're allergic to Oreos," she zinged, reminding me of my severe allergy to chocolate.

Hazel was the backbone of our community. She knew everyone who was anyone in town on a first-name basis, and her Sunday porch storytelling crowd was still going strong. Hearing about Cassie and Kyra must have humiliated her in front of her fans, but Hazel was no saint, and she had her own share of enemies.

Hazel had married five times in the years I was growing up. She had the bad habit of changing my last name whenever she married another man. In time, I learned not to attach much significance to my last name. Kent seemed to have been her favorite, seeing as they remarried twice. Each time she remarried him, she changed my name back to his. I thought he was the best of the lot. He worked for Boeing for thirty-seven years and he was the one who could put up with Hazel's belligerent attitude.

When I was a kid, I remember one black family who tried to settle there. Our community had one police officer, a Smokey and the Bandit sheriff who tended to look the other way whenever he saw fit. Hazel and the sheriff were childhood friends, and the sheriff was an active member of Hazel's grapevine community. The black family lived in town for thirty days and then packed up and left. I was surprised they lasted that long and suspected Hazel had something to do with their hasty retreat.

I knew Hazel regretted adopting me. She voiced her disappointment in me as far back as I could remember. I did not fit the mold that she had created for me. According to Hazel, it was her way or no way. I was stubborn, and we argued a lot. She spanked me all the time, and when I asked why, she would say, "It's just in case you do anything wrong and don't get caught for it."

I got a belt for Christmas when I was six years old. I wore it every day but not around my waist. I had imprints of that belt on my butt every single day. Owning a belt held a whole new meaning to me after that.

When Hazel married Kent, the Boeing man, we moved onto the same property with Hazel's mother, my grandma Marie. Grandma Marie saved my life. As long as Grandma Marie was around, I was unharmed. But when she was away,

I caught hell—a polite way of putting it. My adoptive brother could do no wrong in Hazel's eyes.

Grandma Marie was the only real mother figure I had, and I loved every single gray hair on her head. Dark-eyed and heavyset, she always wore an apron. She was an extremely loyal American and expected all her sons and grandsons to serve in the military.

Grandma Marie had friends of other races, but she insisted that they "know their place." She drew the line with Asians because she saw the men in her family fight against them and die in the Pacific, Korea, and during Vietnam. She took it personally and was never able to forgive them.

My grandma cooked, canned, knitted, and sewed better than anyone in our town did. She taught the young women how to take care of their men. I missed her as I drove away from Hazel's house. She would have listened to me. She would have known how to smooth things over, but she was gone, and I was a grown man with children of my own. Nothing had changed between Hazel and me. I doubt it ever would.

On the way to pick up Gabe and Jason, I reminded myself that a large part of me was still racist. I had become two men, depending on the situation. One was a tolerant and understanding man; the other I labeled as my "white-man mode." Depending on who I was with, I flip-flopped back and forth, not completely loyal to anyone, a traitor to all, mostly myself.

Chapter 12

"Is Santa going to leave gifts for Kyra too, Dad?" Jason asked.

"I expect so," I told him.

"Even if Kyra has been naughty this year?" Gabe asked.

"Well, now, we'll have to wait and see, won't we?" I said.

The doorbell rang. I was in the kitchen, taking care of what little was left to do for our dinner. Gabe opened the door and let Cassie and Kyra in. Kyra rushed into my arms, squealing, "Jeffie Weffie!"

"Merry Christmas, Kyra," I said, swinging her around a couple of times. She giggled and said, "Do it again, Jeffie Weffie!"

Gabe grabbed my left leg, and Jason grabbed the right. While I walked around the room with the kids hanging on me, Cassie carried in the presents, but there were more gifts than what we had bought together.

While the kids were washing for dinner, I asked, "Hey, what's with all the additional presents?"

"They're for the kids. It's what Christmas bonuses are all about," she said.

"You shouldn't have spent so much money on Christmas," I scolded.

"Yeah, I suppose you go all out for dinner like this all the time," she replied.

I served dinner. Kyra was so wound up about Christmas that it was difficult to calm her down enough to eat. After dinner, I kicked Cassie out of the kitchen and cleaned up. As I dried the last dish, an idea came to me.

Candy Cane Lane was a neighborhood street in Seattle where the residents decorated to the hilt every Christmas. The houses, built in the 1920s, were Victorian with wraparound porches. The families would wave as onlookers streamed by. Ever year there was bumper-to-bumper traffic. It was faster to get out and walk. I waited for the time to suggest that we end the evening at Candy Cane Lane.

We opened gifts. Kyra got clothes, books, and art supplies. She was obsessed with drawing, and Cassie encouraged it. Cassie saved them all.

Next, Kyra opened her gift from me, a crystal bear necklace. She had me clasp it around her neck. She loved it. She kept running into the bathroom, admiring her new necklace in the mirror. From that day on, Kyra wore it every day and developed the habit of fingering the crystal bear whenever she was lost in thought. She did not get many toys, but she did get games, dolls, and stuffed animals.

Cassie opened her gifts next and gasped when she saw the pearl-and-diamond necklace from me. I laughed when she followed Kyra into the bathroom, stood in front of the mirror behind Kyra, held up her hair, and waited for me to clasp the necklace around the bare nape of her neck. I kissed her neck softly.

"Jeffie Weffie is kissing Mommy!" Kyra shouted as she ran down the hall.

"Ugh!" the boys shouted. They tumbled over each other, pretending to strangle themselves.

Cassie vowed never to take the necklace off, even while showering or sleeping. I also gave her a new fleece-lined waterproof jacket.

"Now you can get rid of that awful baseball jacket," I said.

"I think I'll keep it as a souvenir," she said, winking at me.

Cassie and Kyra opened the last gift together.

"Mommy, it's a TV!" Kyra shouted. "Is it ours? May we bring it home with us? May I watch cartoons?"

"Yes, it's ours, and yes, you may, honey," Cassie said.

Little arms wrapped around my neck and hugged tight.

"Thank you, thank you, thank you, Jeffie Weffie," Kyra said. She planted little kisses all over my face. "I love you, Jeffie Weffie," she said.

It was the voice of an angel. I realized that I had fallen in love with the little girl. Way down deep inside, I purred like a cat.

The boys got Atari games, Lego kits, and dominoes. Jason loved to spend long hours arranging falling domino patterns. Cassie gave the boys matching Seahawks sweatshirts with a picture of the players on the front. She gave them board games and car models. The model car kits she bought were too complicated for the boys at their ages. Later, I put them in the closet to give to them when they were older.

It was my turn. I opened Cassie's gift first. It was a box of cigars, though I had never smoked a cigar around her.

"How did you know I liked cigars?" I asked. She grinned impishly.

I unwrapped one of the cigars and smelled it, breathing in deeply. It was a high-quality cigar. Cassie said that nuns made them and tied knots on the end by hand. The cigar store in Smith Tower was the only place in town that I knew of where you could buy this brand of cigar. I guessed that they were fifteen dollars each.

Cassie lived near poverty level, but she knew all about superior-quality cigars. I was falling for a secretive woman but I would not pry. She would tell me about her past when she was ready. Until then, I put it out of my mind.

"I have an idea," I said. All heads turned in my direction. "Let's go to Candy Cane Lane!"

Kyra jumped up and down along with the boys. She knew nothing about Candy Cane Lane, but it had to be good since the boys were ecstatic about going.

"Candy Cane, Candy Cane, Candy Cane Lane," Kyra sang, dancing around the room.

I brought the box of cigars with me to Candy Cane Lane. We got out of the car and walked, as planned. I lit a cigar and puffed on it once or twice. "This is very good, Cassie," I said.

"May I taste it?" Cassie asked.

I handed the cigar to her.

She kissed me, put the cigar back in my mouth, ran her tongue around her lips, and said, "Hmm, good."

I leaned close to her and whispered, "I guess you realize what you just did to me."

"No, what?" she giggled.

I raised an eyebrow, laughed, and grabbed her hand. We walked down the lane arm in arm with the kids dancing around us. At that moment, I finally understood what it meant to experience the magic of Christmas.

Cassie and Kyra accompanied me when I drove the boys back to their home. Jen was standing in the doorway when we drove up. The shock on her face was unforgettable. Hazel's grapevine had apparently not made it to Jen's house.

If looks could kill, Cassie would have perished on Jen's doorstep, but Cassie killed Jen with kindness. She unloaded the presents and carried them into the house while I carried the sleeping boys in, one by one, and tucked them in their beds. Jen never saw Kyra, as she was asleep in the back seat.

"Hello, Jennifer, I'm Cassie Baker. What a lovely home you have," Cassie said sweetly.

Jen said nothing. She didn't look in Cassie's direction at all. Instead, she glared at me. She never said a word while we were there. It was petty and immature of me, but the look on Jen's face was a priceless moment for me, and Cassie knew it.

At Cassie's place, I carried all the gifts in except for the television, which we left at the condominium, as it was too big to fit in her Hyundai.

I held Cassie in my arms until Christmas Eve turned into Christmas morning. She was part of me, as essential as my arms and legs. I could not turn back now, even if I wanted to. It was the happiest Christmas of my life.

Chapter 13

I spent Christmas Day at Abbey's house. We celebrated the old-fashioned way. The tradition for Abbey's family was to draw names for gifts. Aunt Sis drew my name this year. She gave me a light-blue Polo shirt with white trim around the collar. Stacey said it matched my blue eyes.

I gave Abbey a white halter dress, size zero, the one she had been eyeing for months.

"Somebody's been paying attention," she said.

Matt and I watched football after dinner. During halftime, I went to walk alone. I had a lot on my mind.

The next day at the after-Christmas sales, Cassie tagged along while I looked for a wedding gift for my close friend and schoolmate, Clint Harris.

Clint and I were friends for life. We knew each other in the way that only childhood schoolmates who grew up together could. I trusted Clint with my life but not with my money. He was a legendary poker cheater and card shark.

Clint belly laughed at what he thought was a good ethnic joke. His father was a Korean War veteran, and Clint worshiped him. His dad learned to use racial slurs during the war and taught them all to Clint. We liked to one-up each other with ethnic jokes. That had to stop now. It would prove to be a tough habit to break.

Clint and I were inseparable until Wendy came along. The first time Wendy showed up on Clint's radar, Clint and I were juniors in high school. We were sitting in math class, and it was the first day of the quarter.

"See that girl over there?" Clint asked, nodding in her direction.

"You mean Wendy Walton? Yeah, I see her."

"I'm marrying her."

"She's out of your league, Clint."

"She will be my wife, you'll see."

That was in 1972. Now, seventeen years later, Clint's prediction had come true.

After buying a couple of gifts from Clint and Wendy's gift registry, Cassie and I had dinner together.

"I'm looking for a nicer place to live, but I can't find anything I can afford in the area where I'm living now," Cassie shared.

"I know a man, Tom Calhoun, who is in the property management business. Want me to give him a call?" I asked.

"Sure, thanks."

I called Tom and told him about Cassie and her financial situation. He said he would look around for a new two-bedroom, one-bathroom apartment, clean and nothing fancy. The next morning, Cassie called, breathless with excitement.

"I signed a lease with Tom on an apartment!"

"That was quick."

"It's a nice place with a swimming pool, and I'll have my own a washer and dryer!"

"No kidding."

"And get this. It's in my price range! Can you believe that? Thank you so much for helping me!" she said.

"I didn't do anything," I said.

"Yes, you did. You made it happen."

The apartment location was in a nice part of town. It had a little patio with a view of the skyline of Seattle and great views of the Olympic Mountains. I guessed it rented for $600 a month. Cassie said that Tom let her rent it for $285 a month.

"Nice," I said. My stomach tightened. I raised an eyebrow. Cassie either did not notice or pretended not to. I sent a bottle of Johnny Walker Blue Label to Tom's office, thanking him for his help. The low rent bothered me. Tom was an acquaintance, yet he did this big favor for me? Or was it for Cassie? I waited for Cassie to volunteer the missing details, but she never did.

I had fallen for a mysterious woman with an unknown past. I sensed the danger I was in. I began to think about reconsidering a future with Cassie and Kyra when Cassie sensed my uneasy mood. She moved close to me. Her eyes were on my mouth. She touched my lips with her fingers. Then her mouth was on my mouth. She was irresistible.

Cassie pulled away and said, "What can I do to thank you for your help?"

"You can go with me to the New Year's Eve party at the Space Needle."

"It's a deal."

She kissed me again.

We began meeting each other every day at the Black Angus for happy hour. As the days passed, I told her about my past girlfriends, my marriage to Jen, the divorce, stories from my childhood, and times with Clint. I kept nothing hidden from her. She hung on every word and asked for details. She spoiled me with attention and seemed genuinely interested in my life. The closer we became, the more she avoided talking about her past, but I was in no hurry. I could wait a while longer.

Chapter 14

I found my black tuxedo with the funky seafoam cummerbund in the back of the closet and had it cleaned. It was New Year's Eve, and I was looking forward to spending it with Cassie. I showered, shaved, put on my tails, took one last look in the mirror, complimented myself for looking spiffy. and drove to Cassie's place.

"Mommy, he's here!" Kyra shouted as she opened the door. She took my hand and led me to the bedroom and to Cassie. She wore a solid royal-blue turtleneck dress that went down to her knees and the single pearl necklace I had given her for Christmas. Her high heels were bright blue with black tips. She rarely wore heels except on special occasions. In stocking feet, we were the same height, but in her heels, she was a couple of inches taller than I. I didn't mind. She looked amazing and was incredibly sexy in heels.

"We should do this more often," I said. "You're stunning."

"Mommy, you're so pretty," Kyra echoed. "And you smell good too."

"Right on both counts, Kyra," I said.

"Mommy is wearing a lure," Kyra told me.

"No, honey, Azure," Cassie corrected.

"It smells enticing, like you," I said.

"Mommy, what does enticing mean?" Kyra asked.

Cassie laughed.

"It means I like it a lot and I like your mommy too," I chimed in.

Kyra looked up at me and gave me her famous dimpled smile. It tickled me when she gazed at me with that awestruck expression of hers. Affection poured out of her and onto me. I loved her as if she were my own daughter. It was getting to the point where I could not think of Cassie without thinking of Kyra. It was an all-or-nothing type of thing. I wanted them both in my life.

"What's that behind your back, Jeffie?" Kyra asked, interrupting my thoughts.

She ran around behind me to look, but I whirled around faster than she could run. We spun around the room until she lost her breath giggling. I opened my palms. Kyra stood on her tiptoes to get a good look. I opened the box in my hand and placed a corsage of white rose and pink orchids on Cassie's wrist.

"Pretty," Kyra whispered.

"Hold on. There's one more," I said.

I pulled a tiny wrist corsage with miniature white roses and pink carnations from my coat pocket. "It's for you, Kyra." I said as she gasped.

I got down on my knees and took her little hand in mine. I slipped the flowers on her wrist. Enchanted by the flowers, she carefully moved near Cassie, never taking her eyes off her flowered wrists.

"Look, Mommy, I got one too," she whispered.

I escorted Cassie to the car with one arm and carried Kyra in the other with her arm still sticking straight out.

Cassie gave me directions to her parents' house. I was about to discover more about Cassie's past. We drove through an affluent neighborhood in Bellevue, a large multimillion-dollar gated community. Each estate had either tennis courts or a swimming pool. Cassie directed me to one of the estates with tennis courts. "That's it," she said.

The front lawn was lush and of putting-green quality. I hid the shock I felt from Cassie.

Poor Cassie, rich parents … this is all wrong.

Kyra walked down the long sidewalk and climbed the stone steps to the front entrance, careful not to crush her wrist corsage. She cupped her hand around her eyes and peeked through the ornate beveled-glass panels. She pushed the doorbell. Cathedral chimes rang out.

A tall, thin, balding man appeared. His voice was gentle. "Hello, Kyra," he said as he bent down to shake her hand.

"Hi, Grandpa," Kyra said. She held her flowered wrist out for him to see. He smiled but did not comment. She skipped past him into the foyer and disappeared into the house.

"Hello, Cassie," he said.

"Hi, Dad."

They hugged and stiffly patted each other on the back.

"Come in, please," he said looking from her to me. "I'm Noah Baker."

"Hello, Mr. Baker. I'm Jeff Green."

We shook hands. His grip was cautious but pleasant. He told me that he was a commercial airline pilot for Northwest Airlines. I mentioned my stepfather's association with Boeing.

Kyra reappeared, accompanied by a middle-aged woman. She was stocky, maybe five feet three at the most, with short dark hair, stern gray eyes, and a heavily tanned face. She had the posture of a five-star general. Kyra again lifted her wrist corsage and said, "See, Grandmother? Mommy has one too."

"This is my wife, Madelyn," Noah said. "We call her Maddie."

"How do you do," Madelyn said formally.

Both parents were dressed in Dockers and Polo shirts. Noah explained that they had spent the afternoon at the country club, playing eighteen holes of golf with their best friends, Glen and Margie Jenson. I recognized the name Glen Jenson. He was a well-known local celebrity, a popular newscaster who worked for the highest-rated television station in Seattle.

"Hello, Mom," Cassie said. "This is Jeff Green."

I reached out to greet her with a handshake. She did not respond. It was an awkward moment for me as well as Cassie.

"Are you coming in?" Noah asked.

"No, Dad, we're running late," Cassie said.

"Be careful, Cassandra; it's foggy out," Madelyn said.

"Thanks for keeping Kyra overnight," Cassie said. "I'll pick her up tomorrow morning."

"Ten sharp," Madelyn said.

"I'll take good care of your daughter, Mr. and Mrs. Baker," I said.

Noah smiled, and Madelyn stiffened. When we left, I felt as if we had escaped. I was happy to be out in the cool, moist night air again.

On the way to the Space Needle, Cassie talked about her family briefly. "I borrowed this dress from my sister, Jane. She is a flight attendant and travels a lot. Mitchell, my oldest brother, is a maritime attorney. His practice is in Tacoma. My youngest brother, Aaron, works as a branch manager for Bank of America. That's about it," she said.

"Your mother clearly did not like me," I said.

"It's just the way she is, Jeff. Don't take it personally," she said. "But let's not spoil New Year's Eve with talk of family."

The Space Needle was not visible until it was right in front of us. The fog was thick, and it was raining. I handed my keys to the valet, slipped him a twenty-dollar bill, and requested that he park my BMW nearby. We walked to the entrance at the base of the tower. Cassie squeezed my hand.

"Is anything wrong?" I asked.

"No," she said, not looking at me.

I took her arm and led her into the elevator. She broke away from me and made her way into the center of the elevator, surrounding herself with people on all sides. She was quiet but nervous on the way to the top. The waiter led us to our reserved table. The Seattle city lights twinkled like stars in the rain and fog.

"Come see the view," I said.

"I can't," she said. I'm afraid of heights."

"Does that include elevators?" I asked.

She nodded. "If you don't mind, I am going to sit with my back to the window.

"Would you like to dance?" I asked, thinking she would jump at the chance to get away from the window.

"Not right now, maybe later, maybe, well, okay, let's dance."

On the dance floor, she clung to me like a baby bird that had fallen out of its nest. We danced, but she was too nervous to enjoy it. I led her back to our table. Again she turned her back against the window. Ear-splitting music from the live band made it difficult to hear each other. Cassie cupped her hands around her mouth as she shouted something. I shrugged my shoulders and mouthed, "I can't hear you."

She pantomimed drinking a cocktail. I nodded and waved a waiter over. The server handed Cassie a party hat, a tiara with white feathers and rhinestones. She ordered a cosmopolitan and gulped it down. She ordered another one. She relaxed and began to lighten up. As the evening progressed, she drank a bit of everything and was more than a little tipsy.

The countdown to midnight began. I pulled her onto the dance floor and into my arms. I kissed her as the band played "Auld Lang Syne." Balloons dropped from the ceiling. We kissed through it all. We were six hundred feet above Seattle, surrounded by a cloud of fog and fireworks. Cassie caught her falling tiara and laughed. She held on to the tiara and wrapped her free arm around my neck. She arched her back and swung her body around me, her hair hanging down, tickling my hands. She was beautiful, sexy, mesmerizing, and clearly drunk.

When the countdown ended, fireworks exploded over the city. Explosions went off inside me. Colored fog blinked on and off in the mist.

"Happy New Year, Cassie," I said, holding her close. I wanted to take her somewhere secluded and kiss her all over, but she was dizzy with intoxication. It was time to go home, and there was no other way down but the elevator. Cassie clenched my arm as we descended.

"I'm scared, I'm scared, I'm scared," she mumbled.

When the doors opened, she rushed out into the lobby and through the front entrance, banging the glass door.

A handful of state patrol officers noticed her. I recognized a couple of them from my days with the department and said hello.

Cassie walked up to the group and said, "Jeff's drunk, and I need a cab."

The troopers laughed. One of the men said, "The cabs are right over, there ma'am."

I spotted our car parked right next to the cab. "If the lady wants a cab, I'll get her a cab," I said.

After paying the valet, I led Cassie to the car. It worked. She climbed into the seat, thinking it was a cab, and fell over onto her side. I took off my tuxedo jacket and rolled it into a pillow for her head.

We drove home. Traffic had stalled somewhere ahead on the 520 bridge, and by the time we reached the other side, my bladder was full.

I looked for the first open place and spotted an ESSO station to my right, but it had closed. I could not wait any longer and pulled into the station. Cassie was out cold. I locked the doors and walked around to the used tire rack. I was enjoying relief when a car showed up.

"Stop. Now come out slowly," shouted a man through the PA system in his car.

I zipped up my pants.

The police officer got out and walked to the front of his car with his headlights blaring at me. He put his hands on his holstered gun.

"The station is closed, sir," he said. "What are you doing here?"

I told him my story starting from when I needed to go pee until he shined his flashlight on my unfinished business. I told him my girlfriend had too much to drink and had passed out in the car.

"How much have you had to drink, sir?" he asked.

"Two Baileys and a glass of champagne over a four-hour period," I said.

"So, you're not impaired, right?" he said.

"Right," I said.

He walked over to our car and shined his flashlight in the front seat.

"You are taking her home with you?" he asked.

"No," I said, "I am taking her to her house."

"Happy New Year," he wished me and left.

It seemed strange, but the officer did not ask me for identification. When we got to Cassie's place, I could not wake her up. I retrieved my wet tuxedo jacket. Cassie had slobbered all over it.

I found her purse and her house keys and let myself in. I went back to the car and tried to wake her again, but she did not respond. I carried her inside and laid her down on the bed, slipped off her heels, and placed her pearls on the table in the other room. Her tiara managed to survive the evening, missing a feather or two. I hung it on the bedpost near her head and wondered if she would remember where it came from the next morning. With some effort, I rolled her onto her stomach and covered her with a blanket, not wanting her to get cold during the night.

"Happy New Year," I whispered. I kissed her good night and locked the door behind me.

I took the long way home to think. This was a night of extremes. I hoped that Cassie would remember at least part of the evening. I thought about the contrast in lifestyles between Cassie and her parents and between her parents and me. There had to be a story there. I braced myself for 1990.

I got home at two o'clock in the morning and looked forward to spending the next day alone, watching football.

Chapter 15

On the first workday after New Year's Day, Cassie began leaving little love notes in my truck. We saw each other every day that week, meeting at the Black Angus after work. Cassie talked about her mother for the first time since the party. "You were right about Mom," she said. "She disapproves of you."

"I'm not surprised," I said.

"It's just like Mom to think the worst before getting to know you," she explained. "Give her some time, Jeff. She'll come around."

Cassie had to be out her garage apartment by January 15. I rented a truck to move her things and reminded Cassie that it was my turn to have the boys for the weekend.

"Mom's going to keep Kyra. She can keep the boys too," Cassie said.

"Are you serious? You just told me she didn't like me," I said.

"I'm sure it will be okay."

I hesitated and then said, "Well, then, if you say so. You know her better than I do."

Noah's car was gone when we arrived at her parents' house. The live-in housekeeper told us he had gone to pick up the rental shampooer to clean the carpets at the garage apartment. I was relieved that Madelyn did not greet us at the door. The housekeeper herded the kids inside and shut the door.

Cassie and I focused on the move. She was excited about the new apartment. Noah was waiting for us when we backed into the driveway at the garage apartment.

"I've got cleaning up covered on this end," he said. "All you have to do is move Cassie's things, and I'll do the rest."

We packed boxes and moved everything into the truck. When we were done, most of the truck's cargo area was still empty. We could have easily made the move with a couple of trips in my truck.

"Let's go! I can't wait to get out of here," Cassie said.

"Give me your keys, Cassie," Noah said. "I'll make sure the creatures who own this place get them."

Moving Cassie's few things into the new apartment was like parking a Volkswagen in the empty parking lot at Qwest Field. In an hour, we were done. Our voices echoed off the walls of the unfurnished rooms.

When we dropped by to pick up the kids, Madelyn was sitting at the kitchen table, sipping a cup of coffee.

"The children have been fed," she said. The boys said later that they ate peanut-butter-and-jelly sandwiches.

We heard the sound of little feet running up the basement stairs and stepped into the hall to greet them. Jason and Gabe shouted, "Daddy! Daddy! Daddy!"

"Daddy! Daddy! Daddy!" Kyra said as she followed behind them.

"Do you think your mother heard that?" I whispered.

"My mother is neither dumb, stupid, nor deaf," she said defensively. From the sour expression on Madelyn's face as we walked back into the kitchen to say good-bye, she had indeed overheard.

"Thank you for watching the boys, Mrs. Baker," I said.

"It's okay, Jeff. You can call her Mom," Cassie said.

"My name is Madelyn. My *friends* call me Maddie," she said, making it clear that calling her *Mom* was off limits. It was a short, curt conversation. We hurried the kids through the door and left in a flash. That woman could make it snow in Puerto Rico.

"You're quiet," Cassie said. "Is anything wrong?"

"No, nothing," I said but was thinking *Your mother is a bitch*.

We stopped at Chuck E. Cheese on the way back. Cassie disappeared and came back with a pitcher of beer. "Can we talk? I know something is bothering you."

We drank the beer and chatted, but I knew better than to tell her what I really thought of Madelyn.

When I got home, there was a message on the machine from Abbey. I missed Abbey. We rarely talked since Cassie came into my life. I called her back right away.

"She's not home, Jeff," Matt said.

At six the next morning, the phone rang. "How've you been?" Abbey asked.

"What are you doing up?" I said. "It isn't nine o'clock yet. Go back to sleep."

"Not until you give me an update, stranger."

I caught her up on Cassie's mother and the new apartment.

"Don't mess with Mom," Abbey said.

"Yeah, I got that," I said.

"Listen, Jeff. You should let Cassie go shopping in your storage place. Remember the old furniture from your apartment that didn't match the modern theme? It's all there. Aren't you paying monthly storage fees for stuff you'll never use again?"

"Thanks for the reminder, cousin. It's good to hear your voice again," I said.

The next day I took Cassie to the storage place. She chose my old dining room set, a couch, a recliner, two floor lamps, two end tables, a coffee table, and an entertainment center.

"Do you want my old bedroom furniture, even though I don't have a mattress and box spring?" I said.

"Do you think I need a bigger bed?" She smiled wickedly.

"If you ever get a boyfriend who wants to spend the night, it might come in handy."

"You rat," she said, slapping my chest playfully.

We moved furniture in, and the echoes disappeared. She hugged me. "It feels like home."

We continued seeing each other every day throughout the month of January, although I was busy at work juggling several big projects.

Cassie had become the center of my world. I stopped keeping up with current events, stopped calling friends, and stopped checking on my boat regularly. Between work and Cassie, I had no life, except when the boys visited every other weekend. I stopped hunting and fishing and never thought to call Abbey or Clint. Life was full when I was with Cassie and an empty void when away from her.

Chapter 16

"Cupid shot his arrow, and damn it, he missed," read the Valentine's card I picked out for Cassie. On the front was a red heart bulging out of a clown's chest. I ordered three dozen long-stemmed roses—pink, red, and white. I had the flowers delivered at three different times during the day at Cassie's office. I bought a hundred heart-shaped helium balloons, drove over to Cassie's workplace during office hours, and crammed all the balloons into her Hyundai, minus three or four that got away when the door opened. I left the Valentine's card propped up on her dashboard.

On Valentine's afternoon, Cassie called, thanking me for the roses. No one else in her office had received a single flower. She said her coworkers got a kick out of the balloons in her car.

After work, I drove by Cassie's office and picked her up. Her dressy clothes were in her car, which she managed to retrieve, letting a few more balloons escape.

At the Japanese restaurant, while the chef chopped and sautéed our dinner on the grill in front of us, I pulled out a romantic card along with a gold bracelet and slipped it under the table and into her lap.

She kissed me and slipped the bracelet on. Three hours later, we ordered dessert. The juice from a ripe strawberry rolled down her chin, and I kissed it clean. We went back to her office to get her car, and while we were there, we divided the roses and balloons equally among her twenty-five to thirty female coworkers.

When I got home, the phone was ringing. "Mom is really pissed, and Kyra is having another tantrum," Cassie said with a panicky voice.

"Take it easy. Tell me what happened," I said.

"Kyra is mad because I stayed out so long. Mom says that we are spending too much time together and that I am neglecting Kyra."

"Do you think we're spending too much time together?"

"No, Jeff, I don't, but it gets worse. I showed Mother the gold bracelet you gave me, and she wouldn't look at it."

"I didn't give the bracelet to your mother, Cassie. As long as you like it, that's enough for me."

"That's really sweet, and you know I love the bracelet, but …" Cassie continued ranting about her mother while I listened. I remembered Abbey's don't-mess-with-Mom comment. She was right again. Madelyn's hold on Cassie was strong, and no amount of interference from me could change that.

I went to bed thinking of the contrast between the woman I knew and loved and the girl who lived under her mother's thumb.

Chapter 17

No one knew my date of birth, not even Clint, and I liked it that way. Thus, I hesitated when Cassie called and said, "I am taking you out for a birthday dinner this weekend."

"You've been snooping," I said. "Who told you about my birthday?"

"I'll never tell," she said.

On Saturday, I bought myself a birthday present: a brand-new Chrysler LeBaron convertible. It was all white with a white top and white leather interior. On the way home, buyer's remorse set in. I parked the convertible in the assigned parking space near the front door. A few minutes after seven, Cassie rang the doorbell. I was expecting a birthday kiss hello, but she was pissed.

"Some jerk parked in your spot, and I can't find a place to park," she said.

"What the hell!" I said, playing along.

"My car is idling," she said.

"Why don't we waste gas in my car?" I said. "I'll find a place for yours."

I parked her car next to my Mazda truck in the guest parking area. Cassie grabbed her purse and headed for the truck. She turned around and saw me standing next to the LeBaron with the door open.

"Why?" she asked.

"It holds more people."

"What's the real reason?"

That's when I realized the true intention behind my gift, the convertible for Cassie, not me. I tossed her the keys, and she jumped in the driver's seat. She drove the convertible with the top down all the way to the restaurant, even though it was below freezing.

That night at dinner, Cassie opened up to me. She told me stories from her childhood, starting with her first memory. She was beginning to trust me. Time flew by, as it always did when I was with her. However, she told her mother she would pick up Kyra at nine. It was now ten.

We hurried back to my condominium. Cassie rushed to her car and drove away without a kiss good night.

Over the next couple of weeks, I was on the road a lot. Work needed my attention, but I stayed in touch with Cassie as well as Abbey.

Abbey's questions multiplied. "What do you know about the family? Are they Catholic? Jewish? What about her past love life? Who's Kyra's father?"

"Whoa, slow down," I said. "Her father is an airline pilot; her mother is a housewife, and they are practicing Catholics." I told her what I knew about the rest of the family.

"Look, I'm sorry, Jeff. I'm just concerned because you know nothing about her past from her high school years to the present, specifically her past love life," she said.

"She hasn't talked about that yet."

"Aren't you curious?"

"Sure, but it can wait."

"Don't wait until it's too late."

"You worry too much."

For the rest of the month, I focused on business clients and projects. In March, the day before St. Patrick's Day, I called Madelyn. "Will you pick Kyra up at school tomorrow afternoon? Cassie and I will drop by and pick her up that evening, if it's okay with you."

"May I ask you what your plan is?" Madelyn said after a long pause.

"I have a surprise for Cassie on St. Patrick's Day. I have already called her boss and asked permission for her to have the day off."

"Cassie can't afford time off from work," Madelyn noted.

"Her boss said yes."

"You shouldn't have asked, but since you did, I'll watch Kyra for you."

"Thanks."

"Let me be clear on this with you, Jeff. I don't approve of Cassie taking time off from work because of an impulsive decision you made for her. Don't put me in this situation again."

I called Cassie early on St. Paddy's Day. "Do you want to have breakfast with me this morning?"

"Sure," she said, "but I have to drop Kyra off at school first."

"How about if I pick you both up? We can drop Kyra off on the way," I suggested.

"Come over," Cassie said.

In front of Kyra's preschool, she hugged me tight, kissed Cassie, and ran toward the school, waving good-bye.

"It's not the same with the boys," I said.

"What's not the same?" Cassie asked.

"Girl hugs and boy hugs," I said. "Don't get me wrong; I love Jason and Gabe. But when we hug, it's more like a handshake. When Kyra hugs me, she doesn't hold back. It's a great feeling. I miss not having a daughter," I said.

"I'll share with you."

"If she'll have me," I said, leaning over to kiss her. "Kyra seems to have stopped pouting. Maybe she's getting used to us being together."

"I think so too," Cassie said.

We drove east on I-90, heading out of town.

"Where are we going for breakfast?"

"Leavenworth."

"What! No way, you lie," she said.

"It's the truth."

"Jeff, turn around right now," she said, a glimmer of anger in her voice.

"It's okay, Cassie."

"No, it's not! It's a three-hour drive to Leavenworth! Turn around now, or I will be late for work! I can't lose my job!" she shouted.

"You won't lose your job," I said casually. "You're off today. I cleared it with your boss."

"Still, we can't do this. I have to pick up Kyra after school."

"Calm down. I called your mother. She is going to take Kyra home with her after school today."

"You called Mom?"

I nodded.

A few minutes later, she said, "My, my! You've been busy, haven't you? Did you tell Mom what we were doing?"

"I told her that I had a surprise for you. She didn't ask for details, and I didn't volunteer them."

Two and a half hours later, we pulled into Leavenworth, a quaint Bavarian mountain village in the Central Cascade Mountains. I had hoped to see the village shops along Front Street under a blanket of snow, but this was a rare warm day in March, and the streets were wet with snowmelt. We ate breakfast at a Dutch café and browsed the shops afterward.

We drove another two hours to Lake Roosevelt on the Columbia River above Grand Coulee Dam. I packed a picnic lunch before leaving town and hid it in the trunk. Lake Roosevelt was a huge lake, 150 miles of water stretching all the way to Canada, with sunny, sandy beaches and basalt canyons. Cassie had never been there before.

"Wow!" she said as she looked at the glacier-scarred cliffs. "It takes my breath away."

We picnicked on the beach, played in the sun, and chased each other on the sand until I was tipsy with lust.

"Let's take the long way home and prolong the day," I said. I took the top down on the convertible. The wind lifted Cassie's hair like a frilly black petticoat. The sunshine lit up her face, and her freckles multiplied. She looked as free as a bird soaring in the wind, very different from the grown woman who remained trapped under her mother's thumb.

We passed a shantytown and decided to look around. Run-down buildings lined a single main street. The countryside was speckled with a handful of house trailers and an old Victorian home with caved-in porch. We passed a barn with a rust-covered sign on the front door that said *Tavern*.

"I've been in a bar but never in a tavern. What's the difference?" Cassie asked.

I turned the convertible around and drove back to the tavern, seeing as it was only three in the afternoon.

"It's a ghost town," she said.

"Well, let's go and meet some ghosts. Whaddya say?" I laughed, escorting her inside.

Two faded pool tables sat beside a long bar counter. A group of women wearing braless tank tops with pink sponge rollers in their hair sat at the counter, smoking and drinking beer.

A hard-faced, middle-aged woman spotted us. Her shoulder-length, overly dyed hair looked brittle like black hay. Red lipstick smeared her mouth way past the boundaries of her thin lips. A cigarette balanced on her bottom lip and dangled dangerously when she spoke.

"What'll it be for you, folks?" she asked, not looking up from her pad.

"A couple of glasses of house beer," I said.

"Coming up," she replied.

Hanging all around the room were flycatchers swirling from the current of ceiling fans. Cassie asked about the restroom. The woman lifted her nicotine-stained finger and pointed to the far corner of the room. Cassie excused herself.

I looked back toward the bathroom. Through a large gap near the bottom of the door, I saw a pair of familiar-looking tennis shoes. The base of the toilet was in clear view. Cassie's jeans dropped down around her ankles. I hurried to the bathroom door, took my jacket off, and shielded the view from onlookers. The toilet flushed. Cassie opened the door and realized why I was standing there. She blushed and thanked me.

Our beers were waiting for us back at the table. Cassie took one sip and wrinkled her nose. "No more, thanks," she said.

I paid the tab. As we were leaving, a yellow school bus pulled up in front of the tavern. The driver opened the bus's stop sign. The braless women in hair rollers moved toward the exit and waited inside the door. A group of young kids spilled out of the bus and into the tavern. Minutes later, the whole bunch disappeared around the corner. We laughed about the happy hour moms and wondered if it was a daily occurrence.

Years later, I went back to the spot where I thought the tavern was, but it was gone, along with its quirky inhabitants.

On the way home, Cassie moved over on the bench seat close to me. She leaned her head against my chest and took a nap. I wrapped my arms around her, protecting her from the wind. This felt good and right. She woke up as we were driving past North Bend. It was six in the evening.

"What time did you tell Mom we'd pick up Kyra?"

"I didn't give her a time," I informed her.

We were about to pass the Lake Sammamish exit, the turnoff that led to my condominium. Cassie suggested that we exit and drive around the lake.

"Are you sure you didn't tell Mom a specific time?" she asked.

"I'm sure."

"I think it would be fun to go by your place and have a drink," Cassie said.

"I like the way you think," I said.

At the condo, I uncorked a bottle of late-harvest white wine. Cassie took a sip. "Perfect," she said.

I stepped into the kitchen to slice some fruit and cheese. When I returned, Cassie had disappeared.

My bedroom door opened. Cassie stood in the doorway, wearing one of my solid-colored dress shirts and nothing else. The light from the bedroom lit up the cotton and turned her body into a silhouette, her nipples stiff against the starched cotton. The rest of the shirt draped open, revealing darker areas that made me ache for her.

She moved closer, took my hand, and led me down the hall and into the bedroom. We made passionate love. Lying in each other's arms in the afterglow, I felt a deeper intimacy between us. I fell into a peaceful sleep, knowing that this amazing woman would be beside me when I awoke.

Sometime later, Cassie shot straight up in bed. "Oh, my God. What time is it?"

I glanced at the clock on the nightstand. "It's eleven."

We threw our clothes on like a couple of soldiers in basic training, and in five minutes we were out the door and speeding along I-90 toward Bellevue.

At eleven twenty, Noah Baker opened the front door.

"Thank you for waiting up, Dad," Cassie said. "I'm so sorry we're late."

"Mom's not happy," he said.

"Where is she?" Cassie asked.

"She's gone to bed," Noah said.

I said good night and drove the long way home, bracing myself for the downhill slide.

Chapter 18

For the next two weeks, I was on the road constantly, meeting with business clients. I called Cassie every night. She filled me in on what happened with her mom the next morning after our first time together.

"She gave me hell, Jeff. She said I could do better than you. I told her she was being unfair and that she had not even taken the time to get to know you. I begged her to give you a chance."

"Am I not rich enough for her? Is that it?"

"I don't know, maybe. She did try to persuade me to start dating some of Mitchell's attorney friends, but I reminded her about the times I had gone out with them. As soon as they found out about Kyra, they disappeared."

"How did you leave things with her?"

"Not good. She won't budge. She said I wasn't making good choices and that if she had to, she would make them for me."

"Maybe what's closer to the truth is that she hates it that I'm helping you stand up on your own."

"Don't talk about Mom that way!" Cassie said. "She's only trying to help me."

"Yeah, she wants to help you right out of my life," I said.

While I was out of town, the news about Cassie and me spread. I started getting messages on my answering machine from people who disapproved of my involvement with an "Oreo" family.

It was difficult not to stay down. When I was with Cassie, nothing else mattered. After a few hours away from her, I began thinking of ways to end it. I thought about calling Abbey, but she would probably tell me that I was in this alone. And I did feel alone. I was a dog chasing my own tail. Cassie would call at night, and I would be back in the land of rainbows and puppy dogs. She was irresistible, and it was maddening.

It was as if God had handed the month of April to me and said, "Here, deal with it." It was a month of daily contrasts: rain and then sun, wind and then calm, flooded rivers and then sprouting trees. April was as bipolar as my current mood swings. It was also birthday month. Everyone close to me had a birthday in April—Clint, Jason, and Gabe to name a few. I knew more than I wanted to know about people who were born under the zodiac sign of the ram. I butted heads with them routinely, and at the same time I loved them passionately and pledged my unending loyalty to them. It was like living close to a hot fire. The warmth of the flames kept me close, but I knew to step away when the fire got out of control, as it invariably did with my Aries people. Thus, I was not surprised to learn that Cassie and Kyra had April birthdays as well.

First up on the April birthday calendar was my friend Clint. I joined him on the first day in April, his birthday, at Smokey Joe's Tavern in Snoqualmie, a picturesque mountain town that sat literally on the edge of the Snoqualmie River. We met every year, same time and place. Smokey Joe's was our favorite haunt as teenagers. Every year we played a round of pool, had a few beers, and reminisced. At some point, we ended up talking about the past year and either cried in our respective beers or slapped each other on the back, whichever was appropriate. No girls were allowed. With everything that was happening in my life, I needed some time with my old friend and was glad to see him when he sat down at the bar beside me and slapped me on the back cheerfully.

"You look good, my friend. Your newlywed status must be agreeing with you," I said as I ordered his favorite beer. "This round is on me."

"I'm one happy cowboy, Jeff, but what about you? You look like somebody died. Is it beer-crying time?"

I caught Clint up on recent events. "It's like my life is all about day-to-day crisis lately, and it's wearing me down. I feel like I'm on a roller-coaster ride that will never end."

"Never is a long, long time, buddy. I mean it. What's the hurry, you know?"

After a short period of chatting with Clint, I began to feel like myself again.

"Why couldn't I go with you?" Cassie pouted. "Couldn't you and your friend have made an exception this time?"

"Not a chance. Wendy balked at first too, but she's used to it now."

"Don't count on me to ever get used to being away from you," she said. "I believe in togetherness. You're the one who'd better get used to it."

We had grown much closer. Sex changed things; it always did. Any man who levied that sex was just sex was not only lying to the woman but lying to himself. *Just another lay* was never just another lay, and people who thought so were not as self-aware as they liked to think they were. The biggest lie of all was, "It meant nothing." The truth was more like, "I wish it meant nothing."

The next date on the April birthday calendar belonged to Kyra. She turned four on the third. Madelyn and Noah planned a surprise birthday party for her, but as it turned out, I was the one who was in for a big surprise.

On the way to the party, Kyra asked, "Are Gabe and Jason coming to the party?"

"Not this time, Kyra. They are at their mom's house."

"We need to get the kids together more often. Kyra misses them," Cassie said.

"You'll see the boys soon, Kyra. I promise."

At the Bakers' house, Cassie and Kyra led me through the foyer and into the dining room. Cassie's relatives were there along with some of Noah and Madelyn's friends, including the celebrity TV newscaster and his wife. I was not good at mingling, but I attempted to do so for Cassie's sake.

"Do I hear a Minnesota accent?" I asked a well-dressed gray-haired woman whose breasts sat on her protruding abdomen.

"Why, yes, it is!" she said, extending her hand. "You must be Cassie's Jeff. She speaks highly of you. I'm Rosie Aldridge, also known as Aunt Rosie, though I'm not really Cassie's aunt." Her eyes twinkled, and her double chin jiggled as she talked. She pulled down her glasses to get a good look at me. The unexpected pleasantness from a friend of the Bakers caught me off guard.

"Hello. Yes, I'm Jeff Green. It's a pleasure to meet you, Mrs. Aldridge."

A bald man with a jovial face who was at least a foot shorter than Rosie, with a waist wider than he was tall, worked his way out of the crowd and toward us. "Rosie, dear, you are too Cassie's aunt. And I'm proud to say I'm her uncle Frank. Now, sweetie, introduce me to this young man you have cleverly trapped in your web."

If it was true that somewhere in the world, each of us had a twin, then I was standing in front of Fred and Ethel's twins from *I Love Lucy*. Frank Aldridge shook my hand vigorously.

Frank and Rose put me at ease and charmed me with stories about the old days and life in Minnesota when the Bakers were their next-door neighbors and Cassie was a little girl.

Cassie glanced at me from across the room and winked. I gave her an everything-is-fine look. Frank and Rosie explained that they were very close to the Bakers and loved them like family.

Cassie's brothers, Mitchell and Aaron, dragged me away from Frank and Rose, shoved a beer in my hand, and we talked sports and cars for a while. I found myself enjoying their company.

"If you're good to our sister, we will get along just fine," Mitchell said as he handed me another beer. Aaron nodded in approval. I remembered Cassie's remark that Aaron was the quiet one in the family and Mitchell was the handsome, gregarious one.

"Dinner is served in the dining room," the server said. "Follow me, please."

We followed him into the formal dining room. The table gleamed with sterling silver and fine gold-rimmed china. Cassie and I sat next to Mitchell and Aaron. We waited for Madelyn to take her napkin and then followed suit. I secretly thanked Grandma Marie for teaching me formal table manners.

I leaned toward Cassie and whispered, "Where's Kyra?"

"In the playroom."

"But this is Kyra's birthday party, right?"

"Don't," Cassie said, glaring at me.

A multicourse gourmet dinner followed. Everyone was polite and well-mannered. Madelyn controlled the topics of conversation.

The server cleared our dinner plates and began table preparations for dessert and coffee. Cassie excused herself. She came back a few minutes later with Kyra, who was dolled up in a frilly dress, with ribbons in her hair.

The guests applauded. On cue, Kyra sat at the head of the table in Noah's lap. The server brought in a small white cake with white icing and four burning candles surrounded by white daisies. We sang the birthday song, and Kyra made a wish and blew out the candles.

"Kyra, you can have your birthday cake in the kitchen. We'll open gifts later," Madelyn said.

Kyra followed the server, who carried the cake out of the room. I wanted to be with Kyra on her birthday, not these stodgy grownups. Children's birthdays were about balloons, games, and other kids. In my view, it was an insult to Kyra, and it irked me.

The server returned with an elaborately decorated three-tier cake with ivory buttercream frosting, adorned with real daffodils and other spring flowers. Madelyn mentioned the caterer's name casually. Heads nodded around the table in collective approval. It made me sick to my stomach.

The wife of the news anchor friend singled me out and said, "So, Jeff, where do you live?"

While I considered my response, Madelyn interrupted. "He lives on Lake Sammamish, in a condominium which is entirely unsafe for children. It's too close to the waterfront."

I looked at Cassie. She looked down and listened. Madelyn looked me directly in the eyes. "You know, Jeff, Cassie will expect more than you can possibly give her."

I held her stare.

"It's obvious that you can't adequately provide Kyra with what she needs to know about her heritage. You probably know by now that Kyra can be a handful. You need to realize that there are things about her that you couldn't possibly understand."

Madelyn had me trapped with her biting tongue and her sharp claws. My ears burned as I broke her gaze and focused on my dessert plate.

Noah cleared his throat. "Cassie, dear, do you mind going down to the wine cellar to get our best red?"

Cassie backed her chair and stood obediently.

"Jeff, why don't you help her," Noah said.

Low murmurs began the minute we left the room. With each step down the stairs to the cellar, my mood darkened. I was acutely aware that Bill Gates lived somewhere on the slopes near here. Cassie pulled a bottle of red.

"Do you want to leave?"

It was time to face reality. I was too white for Kyra. Kyra does need a black father. How could I know what it means to be black? How could I help her with her black heritage? I was kidding myself if I thought I could provide Cassie with a wealthy lifestyle. Madelyn had neutered me in front of everyone.

"Yeah, I'm leaving. Get one of your brothers to take you home."

"No, Jeff, we're coming with you. Get your gift to Kyra, and I'll grab her. We'll meet you at your truck."

Cassie went upstairs with the bottle of wine while I crept into the den and retrieved the bicycle I had bought for Kyra and carried it to the truck. Cassie and Kyra were waiting for me.

It dawned on me that I never had a real relationship with a mother, adopted or biological. So, how could I judge what was normal behavior between Cassie and her mother? Maybe Madelyn behaved the way a normal mother would. How was I to know? Like a meteor hurling through the atmosphere and landing on my car, crushing it with me underneath, my thinking dropped to the lowest point since Cassie and I met.

I was a silent on the way home. The same old battle raged inside me, and it looked like the bad guys were going to win.

"Are you okay?" Cassie asked.

"Yeah," I lied.

I dropped Cassie and Kyra off at their place, left without kissing either of them good-bye, and drove straight home, the shortest way possible.

There was a message from Danny, an old acquaintance who occasionally had attended antique car shows with me.

I stopped hanging out with him when I found out that he dealt drugs on the side and that my ex was one of his clients. Dan eventually cleaned up his act and worked for the biggest telephone company in town, where his father-in-law was manager.

"Hey, Jeff, this is Dan. How's that Oreo thing working out for you?" He snickered and hung up.

I sat down in my easy chair and tried to sort out what had happened. Later, I called Abbey and told her about the party.

"Life's a bitch, Jeff. If you want to be with Cassie, it's going to be tough. It's a shame you didn't defend yourself at the party."

"I love it when you're mean."

"Look, I'm serious. *You* get mean for your own sake. You're going to need it."

Chapter 19

The month of April was not even halfway through, and I wondered what else was in store for me. I also realized that the boys needed me to focus on them and their birthdays. Jason's was on the tenth and Gabe's on the thirteenth. Since their birthdays were so close together, I thought they would be a lot alike. I was wrong. Gabe, the oldest, was dark-haired and dark-skinned like his mother. His hazel eyes were bright, curious, and at times, searching and wanting. Friends and family told me that he had facial features like me. Jason, on the other hand, had blue eyes and fair skin like me but resembled Jen.

He was easy to figure out, or maybe it was easy for me because he thought the same way I thought. In any case, he was perfectly happy with the simple things in life, and he had a keen sense of humor. I always enjoyed my time with the boys. We had a great time together.

It was not in my nature to stay down, no matter what Abbey had said or what Madelyn had done. As a result, on Easter Eve morning I was at Marymoor Park with Cassie, Kyra, and the boys. I was a walking dead man without Cassie. The only time I felt alive was in her presence, hence my inclination to keep trying to make it work.

Our plan to give all three kids bikes for their birthday worked out well. Again, I saw the five of us as a family as we biked together through the park. It was all it took to boost my spirits.

It was a sunny, cool day, perfect for the ride. The boys and Kyra were in front of us, pedaling as fast as they could go, cycling without hands, doing wheelies, and nearly crashing into each other. Cassie and I stayed in back with one collective eye on the kids and the other on each other. In the thickest part of the forest, Cassie pointed out the wild trillium lining the bike path. We bicycled until hunger overcame us.

"It's official birthday celebration day, boys. You get to pick where we go for lunch."

"Chuck E. Cheese!" they said in unison.

We had the usual for lunch: pizza, tokens, noisy kids, a pitcher of beer for Cassie and me, along with some one-on-one time together while the kids played. The conversation was light. Today was all about the kids.

After lunch, my mood continued to soar. We decided to go to the annual Easter egg hunt sponsored by the City of Kirkland. This was no ordinary egg hunt. The city owned a machine that aerated baseball and football field turf. Every year at Easter, the city maintenance crews altered the machine so they could fill it with foil-covered chocolate eggs. Aeration holes, six inches apart, covered the entire playing field, all containing a single chocolate egg. Kyra and the boys scampered all over the field like jumping bunnies. By the time, they were done, all three had chocolate buzzes.

"Today is a good day to meet Hazel," I said.

"Why today?" Cassie asked.

"She'll be in a good mood with all the family there. Today is her annual Easter feast. We can slip in, make our introductions, and head out again without much of a hassle."

"Okay, let's do it."

"Are you sure you're ready to put the shoe on the other foot?"

"It can't be any worse than what we've already been through."

The gravel crackled as we pulled into Hazel's driveway. I recognized nieces and nephews playing in the yard. Gabe, Jason, and Kyra scooted out of the car and joined the kids in a game of kickball.

"See? It's already going well," Cassie pointed out.

"The real test is inside waiting for us. I hope we're not being gluttons for punishment."

Standing at the front door, I wondered why it mattered to me that Cassie and Hazel got along. I grabbed Cassie's hand and knocked on the door.

A robust, ruddy-cheeked, middle-aged woman with tiny eyes and short, curly, graying-brown hair opened the door. She wiped her plump hands on her apron and lifted and wiped the sweat from her face. Her loud voice boomed out into the yard. The kids turned briefly in her direction.

"Don't mind me, kiddos," she said as she waved at them.

"Happy Easter," I said.

"Jeff!" she said as she slapped my back the way she did with her bosom buddies.

"Cassie, this is Hazel Pulaski."

"Hi, Mrs. Pulaski, I'm Cassie Baker. It's a pleasure to meet you."

"What brings you two out this way?" she asked.

"We thought we'd stop by for some of your famous Easter dinner, and I also wanted you to meet Cassie."

"How nice," she said unconvincingly.

We lingered in the doorway and waited for her to invite us in. Hazel's red cheeks grew more intense and round as she smiled. She was smiling a little too much. I knew her well. Underneath the laughing mask was how she really felt. I noticed a slight shadow of expression on her face as our eyes met, and I knew right away that she disapproved, which no doubt would be expressed to me later if I was unlucky enough to be alone with her. I wondered if Cassie saw it too. Then again, Cassie was good at ignoring disapproving expressions from family members.

"What on earth has happened to my manners? Forgive this poor old woman for losing her mind. Please do come in. I'm such a mess! I've been in the kitchen all day," Hazel said with the twinkle of a crocodile ready to pounce on its prey.

"Thank you, Mrs. Pulaski," Cassie said.

"Well, don't just stand there. Come on in and join the party!" Hazel said enthusiastically. She stepped aside to let us in. The brief encounter at the front door was the only time Hazel let Cassie anywhere near her.

Platters of turkey and dressing, sweet potato casserole topped with marshmallows, fresh veggies from the garden, homemade rolls, and apple pie were lined up buffet style on the kitchen counters. We grabbed some plates for the kids and carried them outside.

Kyra and the boys sat beside each other on a bench at the picnic table, hungry, tired, and not interested in coming indoors.

"Dig in, kids. Kyra, wait until you taste Hazel's sweet potato casserole," I said as we placed their plates on the table in front of them.

"I don't like sweet potatoes," Kyra said, holding her nose with her fingers.

"Then eat what you want and leave the rest," I told her.

"Who is Hazel anyway?" Kyra asked.

"My mother."

"Is she your mom?"

"Yes, sort of."

"Do you even have a mom?"

"Kyra!" Cassie said.

"It's okay, Cassie. I'll answer Kyra's question," I said. "Well, Kyra, no, I don't have a super-duper mom like you do, that's for sure. You're one lucky girl."

Kyra beamed.

"I love you, Mommy," Kyra said, hugging her tightly.

Cassie and I headed back inside and fixed our own plates. We found a vacant corner in the dining room and sat down to eat. Everyone seemed to be having a good time except me. I seethed as I watched Hazel avoid Cassie. When Cassie approached, Hazel standing in a huddle with a couple of relatives, she hurried out as if the house was burning down.

Cassie simply did not exist in Hazel's world, though Hazel would never be rude enough to say it directly to her face. Only those who joined Hazel in her beliefs knew what was really going on, and the house was crammed with Hazel's fans. The more Hazel avoided Cassie, the angrier I became.

I walked into the bathroom and tried to calm down. When that failed, I found Cassie, rounded up the kids, and we left without saying good-bye to anyone.

On the way home, after the children fell asleep, Cassie whispered, "Why did we leave so early?"

"It was time to go. I couldn't take it any longer."

"Take what?"

"We'll talk later."

"Okay, fine."

Cassie's eyes were on me as I drove her home. She did that when she knew I was angry.

I promised myself never to return to Hazel's house. I was not going to miss her. After dropping Cassie and Kyra off, the boys and I went back to the condominium, and I put them to bed.

The next day, I called Cassie and asked her to join me for Easter dinner at Abbey's house.

"Sure, why not, as long as Kyra and I get to attend Easter Mass before we go," she said.

"Is it okay if the boys and I tag along with you?"

"Of course, you can come with use. We'd love it," she said, sounding surprised.

The next morning, I managed to get the boys cleaned, fed, dressed, out the door, and on time to pick up Cassie and Kyra for Easter Mass. Cassie genuflected, followed the other members down front, knelt in front of the priest, and took Communion. She was downright peaceful when she returned to the pew to sit beside me.

Meanwhile, Abbey, Matt, their daughter Stacey, and son Doug, attended Easter services at their nondenominational church. After church, we met at Abbey's house for dinner. Stacey and Kyra were instant friends. They played dolls together while the boys roughhoused with Doug.

After dinner, the women cleaned up, covered the leftovers, and washed dishes while the men went outside and migrated to the nearest vehicle with its hood up. This year, Scott, Meredith's boyfriend, brought his new truck, which grabbed the spotlight immediately. Scott was a state trooper, so we spent the rest of the day installing scanners and a CB radio. Eventually the women finished their chores and came out to check on us. Abbey tapped me on the shoulder. "You might want to think about keeping this one."

Abbey had no idea how much I wanted and needed to hear her words of approval. The rest of the family no longer mattered now that Abbey was in my corner. I wanted to tell her how happy she had just made me, but all I could do was grin and say, "Ya think?"

Cassie, Abbey, and Meredith emerged from the kitchen that day as friends. I felt a twinge of jealousy as I saw them approaching arm in arm and exchanging knowing glances in a world that only women inhabit.

As the day ended, I was back in my flying-high mode again, determined that everything would somehow work out between Cassie and me. It was the upside of April. The highs were intoxicating and addictive. I did not want to come down this time.

Later I asked Cassie what she and Abbey talked about.

"It's none of your business, but, well … you."

"I'm not going to beg you for details if that's what you're waiting for."

"Good, because my lips are sealed."

Chapter 20

Cassie opened the door to her apartment, wrapped her arms around me, kissed me, and left her pink peppermint lipstick in my mouth. She was the vision of a wholesome girl about to celebrate her sweet sixteenth birthday, all done up in a pink dress that buttoned all the way down, with matching pink fingernails and the single pearl necklace I had given her around her neck. Her hair curled around her shoulders and back and smelled like baby powder, but her perfume hinted that she was a woman in full bloom whose thirty-third birthday was today.

"Happy birthday, Cassie," I said as I presented her with thirty-three silver-tipped red roses.

"How you spoil me! I have never felt so pampered," she said as she stepped inside to place the roses in water.

"You deserve a day of indulgence," I said, kissing her again, pulling her close to me.

"We better stop, or we'll miss our reservations," she said.

"Then do me a favor and fasten those top three buttons, or I'll have to unbutton the rest."

Cassie slowly buttoned her dress, straightened it, and reapplied her lipstick while I watched. I wanted her even more after she was fully dressed and ready to go.

Hopelessly in love, I sent her flowers once or twice a week. I knew the people at Signature Flowers on a first-name basis, rightfully so. I spent enough money there for the owner to retire early if she wanted to. Sometimes I sent orchids, sometimes spring flowers, many times roses, and on special days, silver- and gold-tipped ones. I got a kick out of wowing her and making her office coworkers envious. Pampering Cassie had become an addiction, but it was not easy for her to accept my generosity. She continued to argue with me when I paid for the sitter. The more provoked she became with my giving to her, the more I wanted to do just that.

We celebrated her birthday at the Kayak Club. We were at the bar, waiting for our table, when I handed her a rectangular box wrapped in silver. She opened it carefully and gasped when she pulled out a full strand of pearls that I purchased at a high-end jewelry store downtown. She draped the strand around her neck, turned around, and waited for me to slip them around her neck. Her eyes were wet when she turned back toward me. There were no admonishments this time. The glow on her face gave me more of a buzz than the Baileys the waiter had just placed in front of me. The pearls blushed against her pink dress and freckled cheeks.

Our eyes locked. I reached for her hand under the bar counter and found it, palm open, waiting for me. Slowly she caressed my fingers as if she held a priceless treasure in her hand. Her pink fingernails trailed up my forearm.

She whispered, "I love you … can't wait to show you how much."

We managed to get through dinner without attacking each other. The server cleared our plates and asked if we wanted to look at the dessert menu.

I leaned over and whispered, "You know you're driving me crazy, don't you?"

She giggled softly.

"Let's get out of here," I said.

Several exquisite hours later, as I drove home, I realized that April was ending with me more in love with Cassie than when the month began, so much in love that I was almost ready to say those three words to her.

As daytime lengthened, the alder trees sprouted in unison and colored the Cascade foothills with lime green. It was May 13, Mother's Day. Reluctantly, Cassie and I had accepted her brother's invitation to attend a family celebration at his house. Mitchell lived in Tacoma in a comfortable trilevel home.

It was the first time I would be in the same room with Madelyn since Kyra's birthday, and I was edgy and quiet. As we drove south on Interstate 5 to Tacoma, the kids turned into little devils. The boys poked Cassie constantly with a coat hanger, played with her hair, unbuckled their seatbelts, and pestered each other. By the time we got to Mitchell's house, my nerves were fried.

When we walked into the house, I turned to Cassie and said sternly, "The kids need a nap."

Without waiting for a response from her, I cornered Mitchell's wife and asked if there was a place for the kids to nap. She led us down to the basement.

The kids fussed about having to take a nap, and their loud whines flipped me out. I did something in the heat of the moment that I wish I could take back. I swatted all three of them on their behinds and shouted, "This is Mother's Day, and you will treat Cassie with respect!"

The room went silent. Kyra started to cry but caught herself. I could count on one hand the times I had been upset enough with the boys to lose it like this. Gabe was the first one to lie down. Jason and Kyra followed his lead quickly. In a few minutes, they were asleep.

I slowly plodded upstairs, drained and not ready to face a roomful of Bakers ready to sink their teeth into me. I went into the living room where the group had gathered. Judgmental eyes stared at me, and I felt guilty as charged. Noah finally spoke.

"You spanked those kids, didn't you?"

I wanted to sneak away and hide. "How did you know?" I said weakly.

"Because your face is as white as a ghost," Noah said.

Mitchell broke through the crowd mercifully and handed me a beer. I drank it quickly and began to calm down. Mitchell and Aaron acted as if nothing out of the ordinary had happened and began talking sports. An hour or so later, the kids appeared fresh from their naps and in a good mood collectively. Kyra sat on my lap, and the boys high-fived me.

From then on, there were no more glitches in the celebration except for Madelyn. I passed by her and said hello. She grunted and looked the other way, which reminded me of something Abbey had said about her that made me laugh, "That woman needs an enema." The image stayed with me for the rest of the day.

On Memorial Day weekend, Cassie, Gabe, Jason, Kyra, and I drove three hours east of Leavenworth to Lake Chelan. I attempted to teach the kids to water ski. Cassie also wanted to learn. The skiing lessons yielded mixed results. The big obstacle with Gabe was that he did not like to get his head wet. I talked him over that hurdle, and after many attempts, Gabe succeeded in staying upright and not falling.

Jason and Kyra were simply too young and not ready to give it a try, but teaching Cassie was a riot. She stood up repeatedly and fell flat on her face. Her bathing suit rode up tucked in unintentional places, embarrassing her. She pretended to be mad and swore revenge when it was my turn to ski. She jerked the boat and took off before I yelled the ready signal. Since my back surgery, I tended to get stiff after a few early takeoffs. I climbed back in the boat. As I toweled off, I heard belly laughs coming from the back of the boat. Cassie and Kyra were in stitches.

"What are you two laughing about?"

"Kyra was looking at your scar," Cassie said, wiping her tears away.

The surgeon must have been daydreaming when he closed me up, because he left a wide scar that went all the way down my spine and disappeared into my swim trunks.

"What's so funny about my scar?"

"It's not your scar that's funny. It's what Kyra said when she saw it," she said and nudged Kyra.

"That's the biggest plumber's butt I've ever seen!" Kyra said, which started them laughing all over again.

I'm sure that person who looked at the plump plumber who bent down to fix the kitchen sink with his rear end popped out of his jeans and coined the phrase "plumber's butt" didn't count on a four-year-old girl saying it, much less knowing what it meant.

"How does Kyra know what a plumber's butt is?"

"Mitchell taught her."

Things were stable for a while. We settled into a happy routine. We met for breakfast before work, and after work we went to happy hour at The Butcher. On weekends, we spent time alone with each other or with the kids. I was vaguely aware that life was going on outside our cozy world, but I was not the least bit interested.

As time passed, Cassie and I decided to make a bold move. We invited Cassie's family, along with Abbey and her family, to my condominium for a Father's Day barbecue.

What was even scarier: they all said yes.

Chapter 21

The time had come for the Bishops, the Bakers, and the Greens to mix and mingle. I lost count of the hours we spent planning and preparing for June 17, Father's Day, and now that the day had arrived, I wondered if Cassie and I had become victims of our own wishful thinking. I had serious doubts that anything positive would happen.

I woke up early with a nervous stomach, and despite reassurances from Cassie that the party would be a success, I held on to the feeling that no matter how much I had planned and prepared, it would never be enough. The day would play out, and all I could do was watch it happen.

The condominium was clean enough to pass a military inspection, the liquor cabinet was well stocked, and the ice chest next to the grill was crammed with a variety of cold beers.

I stepped outside to fire up the grill. The partygoers would be arriving shortly. While I waited for the charcoal to heat, I remembered what Abbey had told me at lunch the day before. "If Cassie is truly what you want, make sure you're strong enough to carry her emotional baggage, plus Kyra's, as well as yours and the boys' with no help from anyone."

The doorbell rang. Cassie greeted Noah and Madelyn, followed by Mitchell and his wife and Aaron and his girlfriend. Minutes later, Abbey, Matt, and their kids appeared, along with her sister, Meredith, and her boyfriend, Scott.

"All the daddies are here, Daddy!" Jason said breathlessly, grabbing my hand, pulling me into the living room, and pointing at the pile of Father's Day gifts on the coffee table.

After a round of handshakes and small talk, I resumed my duties at the grill. Mitchell, Aaron, Matt, and Scott followed me, raiding the beer stash. In the spirit of the moment, I drank a couple of beers too, which settled me down.

Leaving Matt in charge of the grill, I went inside to check on how the party was shaping up. I found it alive and well with a life of its own. Pleased and relieved, I stopped worrying and joined the party.

As the day progressed, I lost count of the drinks I gulped down, not that I intentionally wanted to get smashed. It was more a matter of being distracted with keeping glasses filled and plates full. At least Cassie was not drinking. She rarely drank around her mother.

After dinner, the women rounded up everyone for opening Father's Day gifts in the living room. Drunk and alone in the kitchen, I stood at the sink, washing dishes and trying not to lose my balance, when Madelyn walked in. I felt her staring at me.

"You can throw all the parties you want, Jeff, but you will never be welcome in my family."

She had said the words I had feared the most. I would never measure up. I learned how to control my anger during my years in the military. Unfortunately, I was drunk, fully capable of rage and fury. In a matter of seconds, I was livid.

I forgot my manners and yelled, "Go be a bitch in your own house. You're not going to get away with it in mine."

Before I could unload on her again, Cassie rounded the corner, her face flushed and her eyes glaring at me.

"How dare you call my mother a bitch!"

"But you didn't hear what she said—"

"Whatever she said, you deserved it. I respect my mother, and you will too!"

"But I didn't mean …"

"How could you!" Cassie screamed. She slammed out of the kitchen, pulling Madelyn out with her. By the time I realized what I had done and ventured into the living room to apologize, everyone was gone except Abbey, who was standing over the unopened gifts, her hands on her hips, shaking her head.

She looked at me pityingly. "Matt left with the kids. Cassie, Kyra, and her family stormed off without a word to the rest of us."

"I can explain," I slurred.

"Sure you can, maybe after a pot of coffee."

Abbey's disappointed face was the last thing I remember before passing out. Early the next morning, I woke up in my bed, along with a whopping hangover, unable to remember most of the previous night or how I ended up in my bed. Trying not to move my head quickly, I went to the kitchen, drank a huge glass of water, and made some coffee.

The phone rang painfully. I slowly picked up the receiver. "I don't ever want to see you again," Cassie pronounced.

I was sure I was hallucinating.

"Are you listening to me?" For the first time, I could hear Madelyn in her voice.

"Was it that bad? I don't remember—"

"I can't believe you talked to my mom that way."

"What did I say?"

"You may not remember it, but the rest of us do. You called my mom a bitch. After all the work we put into making it happen, you ruined everything. What kind of man are you?"

"Look, I'm really sorry. If it will help, I will apologize to Madelyn."

"It's too late. It's over."

"You can't mean that, Cassie. I was drunk. It was a mistake. It will blow over."

"Don't call me, don't write me, and don't try to get in touch with me." She hung up.

Just like that, she punched a hole through my chest, yanked my heart out, and left me alone, stunned, and heartbroken.

Chapter 22

Two days after the party, Abbey met me for lunch and told me word for word what went on between Madelyn and me in the kitchen. I felt somewhat justified in saying what I did, but I knew I had to make amends if I wanted Cassie back. I called everyone on the party list who would take my call and apologized for my behavior.

"Don't beat yourself up, buddy," Mitchell said. "We've all had our moments of recklessness while under the influence."

"Lousy timing," Aaron said.

"What's done is done; let it go," Scott said.

Noah and Madelyn refused my calls.

In the days that followed, I called Cassie, but she also refused to talk to me. I missed Cassie, and I wanted her back. I missed Kyra too. I could not sleep and lost my appetite. I shook all over as if I were in full detoxification. A few days would go by, and I would call Cassie again, hoping to catch her in a weak moment, but it never happened.

A week passed. I began a new, complicated project at work and spent a lot of time on the water and cleaning my boat. I fell back into the comfortable, worn ruts of my upbringing. Slowly, painfully, I adjusted to the world again.

There were times when I was glad that the constant emotional turmoil of the recent month was over. I reassured myself that it never would have worked out with us.

The nights, however, belonged to Cassie. I missed the way she looked at me, her face full of love and hope for the future. I missed kissing her freckles, one by one, her perfume saturating my clothes, running my fingers through her hair, and hearing her laugh. I even missed her angry outbursts and her silent, stoic tears. I missed the larger-than-life feeling I had when we were together. So much so that it was difficult to let go of my heartache, since it was all I had left of her. I was lovesick, and it felt worse than being sick with the flu.

After a particularly long night of missing Cassie, I called Abbey to talk, mainly to hear myself say Cassie's name aloud, hoping to summon the image of her face one more time.

"Her eyes did me in, Abbey," I said. "We had chemistry like nothing I had ever experienced."

"Was that it, Jeff? Great sex? Is that why you can't forget her?"

"No—I don't know. It was more than lust, if that's what you mean."

"Other than long legs, a round bottom, and nice boobs, if you don't know why you are in love with somebody, then it's more than sex," Abbey speculated.

She reassured me that life would go on, and she did her part to make it so. She arranged a few dates for me. I went out with three of the women she picked for me, but it was too soon, and I stopped saying yes to Abbey's fix-ups. She meant well, but dating other women only made me want Cassie more.

On July 4, I remembered that Cassie and I had previously made plans to go together to Clint's annual Fourth of July party. I called her one more time and left a message reminding her about the party, but as soon as I hung up, I regretted calling.

A few minutes later, the phone rang. I waited for the machine to take the message while I listened.

My heart skipped when I heard her voice. "How many times do you need to hear me say this? It's over. I will not go out with you. Don't call me again, ever."

After that, I stopped talking about Cassie to anyone, even Abbey. I continued my silent, steadfast loyalty to her and accepted it as part of me that most likely would never see the light of day again.

The next morning, I was up before dawn. It was summertime, and I had promised to take the boys fishing. Gabe and Jason had grown over the summer, which made fishing with them less of a hassle. After I baited their fishing hooks, I leaned back in my chair and relaxed in the sun.

Jason jumped when he felt a nibble on his bobber and scared his fish away.

"Too soon, son," I said. "Wait for it to go under. I'll tell you when to pull."

"Okay, Dad," he said. I reminded them to stay quiet and still while we waited for a bite.

Water bugs skimmed across the smooth surface of the water.

"What's that smell?" Jason whispered.

"When you smell that, it means fish are nearby."

A great blue heron flew over our heads, and the boat wobbled slightly as the boys tried to watch it fly out of sight.

"Dad?" Gabe whispered.

"Yep?"

"Where's Kyra? I miss her."

"Me too, son."

"Can we play with her sometime?" Jason asked.

"Not anymore."

The boys looked up at me, waiting for an explanation.

"Her mom and I had an argument. It didn't work out."

"Oh," they said in unison.

The moment was quickly forgotten when Gabe's bobber suddenly sank under the water and out of sight.

"Pull!" I shouted.

Both Gabe and Jason managed to maneuver a couple of edible fish into the boat, with a little help from me. They watched as I scaled and cleaned the fish. We cooked our fresh catch over the campfire and had a fine meal. We told stories after dinner and slept under the stars. I slept soundly for the first time in a long time and woke up rested. So did the boys. After breakfast, they eagerly took their places in the boat and waited for me to start the motor. We fished until late afternoon and brought a mess of fresh fish home with us.

Years later I would remember that Fourth of July weekend not as a wasted weekend pining over what I had lost but a weekend celebrating the joy of fishing with my boys.

A month passed. When I opened my eyes at five in the morning, I was happy that there was a long summer day ahead and plenty of time after work to take the boat out for a spin.

One morning before work, as I sat at the kitchen table, drinking my first cup of coffee and reading the sports page, the phone rang. "Hi, Jeffie Weffie," the voice said.

"Kyra, is that you, sweetie?"

She hung up. I thought about her all day.

Chapter 23

When I was a young boy with a cut on my knee, I ran crying into the kitchen to Grandma Marie to make it better. She washed my wound and sent me back outside with a kiss, saying my wound would heal faster in the sun and fresh air. Soon I would forget about my cut, and by the end of the day, as far as I was concerned, my knee had healed. From then on, whenever I was physically hurt or felt down, I would go outside and wait for the sun to make it better.

After Cassie left, I spent the rest of summer in the boat out on the lake, under the healing sun. Sunsets were around 9:00 p.m., which left plenty of time after work to devote to the water and then sun. Invariably, my days ended happier than they began.

The rainy season began sometime in October, and most of the locals, including me, welcomed it after several months of dry weather. Like a gigantic warm blanket, gray skies settled over the Seattle area for most of the fall and winter.

Before the rain, though, we enjoyed a long Indian summer and busied ourselves with back-to-school shopping for our kids and last-minute home repairs before the rain set in. It was Jen's turn this year to shop for the boys during the

Labor Day weekend. I looked forward to spending the long weekend enlarging the back deck and installing a hot tub.

On Saturday, I drove to Sears in Bellevue and waded through the crowd of Labor Day shoppers, buying Craftsman tools and other supplies I needed for the deck project. I waited impatiently in a long line at the cash register and paid cash to speed up the process. Glad to be done with shopping, I walked out the front entrance.

Vehicles circled around the full parking lot like hungry vultures waiting for their prey to die so they could move in. A carnival had been set up at the east end of the lot. Sounds of circus music and screaming kids and the smell of hot peanuts and cotton candy brought back my own boyhood carnival memories. Carnivals were as much a part of autumn as falling leaves, birds flying south, and high school football. Out of the cacophony of sounds, I heard the voice of an ecstatic young girl. "Daddy! Daddy! Daddy!"

Her voice disoriented me. It was like running into my UPS delivery person, only he was in plain clothes, out of place, and you could not remember how you knew him.

Kyra ran across the parking lot toward me. In the three months since I last saw her, she had grown much taller, but what shocked me the most was how black she was, as if she had gotten blacker in the summer sun.

I knelt down and spread my arms wide open. She leaped into my arms, bursting with joy as she hugged me tightly. Her unabashed squeals opened doors inside me that I thought I had lost for good.

"Come on, you guys, knock it off." Cassie stood near us, her eyes shining with tears.

"Mom, come here! Daddy will hug you too!" Kyra pleaded with the unguarded honesty of a child.

I stood up with opened arms, and just like that, Cassie walked back into my life.

It was a group hug, a laughing, jiggling mold of Jell-O. All the pain and emptiness of the past months evaporated as if it had never happened. However, it did happen, and we would have to deal with that.

"Mom," Kyra said in a muffled voice somewhere between Cassie and me, "I'll hug the bottom half, you hug the top half." We laughed again.

Cassie looked tenderly into my eyes. I wiped her tears away. We searched each other's faces, and I was relieved to discover that the connection was still there.

"You knew I was here?" I asked.

"No. Kyra spotted you in the crowd just as we stepped off the merry-go-round."

"I'm the luckiest man on the planet that you spotted me, Kyra," I said.

"We're lucky too, Daddy!"

"Can I press my luck and ask you both to lunch?"

"Can we, Mommy? Please?"

Cassie nodded.

We held hands with Kyra between us and strolled across the parking lot to a restaurant in the same shopping center.

Cassie and Kyra excused themselves and went to the ladies' room. My heart pounded as I struggled to make sense of what had just happened.

In an effort to calm myself, I picked up the glass salt and pepper shakers and rolled them back and forth in the palms of my hands until the glass felt warm and smooth. I considered whether our spontaneous reunion was real or just an emotional moment that caught us off guard. I placed the warm salt and pepper shakers back on the table and left them touching each other.

"You look great, Jeff," Cassie said as she and Kyra sat down across the table from me.

"You do too," I said. I wanted to say something like *you look ravishing, more beautiful than my memories of you and I want to kiss you all over and never stop.* I did not want to overwhelm her or seem too eager. So I simply said, "It's been a good summer."

She lifted her eyes and focused on me. "Jeff," she said softly, "I'm so sorry."

"I'm sorry too, Cassie. I hope you'll let me prove that to you."

Kyra giggled and stood up. She grabbed my hand and Cassie's hand and put them together, plopping hers on top of ours.

We caught each other up on our lives during the time apart. Other than tanning by the pool on her days off, Cassie and Kyra visited Noah's father in Arizona. Cassie's sister was there too. Cassie and Grandpa Baker had always been close. He was now in his early nineties and frail, and Cassie wanted to be near him as much as possible.

We eased back into the routine of daily calls and plans to see each other. This was not a fairy tale though. There were still problems.

Chapter 24

Cassie, Kyra, and I celebrated our one-week reunion by having lunch at an upscale restaurant that demanded best table manners. While Cassie and I were in the middle of appetizers and drinks, Kyra stared at an elderly couple nearby. They smiled politely at her and continued their meal. She tried to get their attention.

"Are you Grandpa and Grandma?"

"What are you having for dessert?"

"My name is Kyra, what's yours?"

The couple ignored her.

"Kyra, turn around and leave them alone," Cassie whispered firmly.

Kyra continued.

Cassie looked at me helplessly. By the time we finished our entrees, Kyra had ducked under the table. When I reached down to pull her back up into her seat, she was not there. Cassie excused herself and frantically began looking for her.

"I'm sorry," she said to the elderly couple, "have you seen my little girl?"

In unison, they frowned and pointed to the next table over. Cassie flushed.

"Ruff ... ruff ... ruff." Kyra was on her hands and knees in front of a fully occupied table of four, pretending to be the family puppy.

"Kyra!" Cassie said. "Get up right now! You are being rude to these people during their lunchtime." She picked Kyra up and carried her to our table. "Kyra, I mean it, be still and not a word out of you until we have finished our meal."

Kyra pouted for a few minutes. Then she started crying.

Cassie backed off. "Honey, please."

I had seen this pattern repeatedly with them. We skipped dessert and left. With a clenched jaw, Cassie marched Kyra out to the car and said, "Look what you've done. You've spoiled our celebration."

Kyra whimpered as Cassie buckled her into the back seat, but she held back her tantrum. She seldom had a full-blown meltdown in my presence. After she had fallen asleep, I said, "I don't get it, Cassie. Kyra is Miss Manners when we have dinner with Abbey and Stacey. She mimics Stacey's good manners perfectly."

"It's just kids being kids, Jeff. Gabe and Jason act up too," she reminded me.

It was true. A similar pattern had developed with Gabe and Jason. When we were all together and the boys misbehaved, I had to get rough with them before they would settle down, but if Cassie asked them in a nice way to stop, they would not hesitate to obey her. In time, we learned to cross-parent the children, and for the most part, it worked well.

Cassie got a call from Noah while he and Madelyn were vacationing in Paris.

"Pop isn't doing well, Cassie," Noah said. "We're losing him with each month that passes. I wish I could go to him. Will you go in my place, since I can't be there?"

"Of course, Dad, you know I'd do anything for Grandpa," she said.

Cassie and Noah discussed plans for her trip to Arizona to see Grandpa Baker. After she hung up, she turned to me. "I need to lean on you."

"Go ahead, lean."

"Do you mind if Kyra stays with you until my parents get back from their trip?"

"No problem."

I was nervous about being alone with Kyra with no help from Cassie or the Bakers, but I kept that to myself. I did not want Cassie to worry about Kyra while she was away. It was uncharted territory for me, and I had no idea what to expect. It was the perfect time, though, for a one-on-one trial run.

My doorbell rang. Cassie was running late and needed to rush to catch her flight. She shoved Kyra in the door and gave me a quick hug and kiss. The door closed, and Kyra and I were alone.

My plan was to get Kyra into a routine, to give her some badly needed structure. We hung out on the couch and talked for a while. When things began to warm up between us, we played hide-and-seek. We watched TV together while we ate dinner, using TV trays. Then it was time to get ready for bed. I brushed Kyra's teeth for her, combed her hair, and laid out her pajamas.

"Time to get into your PJs, Kyra," I told her.

"Okay, Daddy," she said pleasantly.

Kyra closed the door and came out a few minutes later, wearing her pink pajamas and fluffy house shoes.

"Did you throw your dirty clothes in the hamper?" I asked without looking up.

"Yes, I did, Daddy," she said.

I read her a bedtime story, kissed her good night, and tucked her in. A few minutes later, I checked on her, and she was sound asleep.

Once the routine between us was established, the rest of Kyra's time with me was a cinch. In fact, we had fun together. She had no temper tantrums, but then again, she did have me all to herself, and she thrived on the attention I gave her.

Kyra was happy, but she missed her mom. We worked around that by calling Cassie every night so Kyra could say good night.

On the third day, Noah and Madelyn called. They were back from Europe. "Thanks for your help, Jeff. Kyra can stay with us now," Noah said.

"It was my pleasure, Noah. It's been fun," I said.

Kyra and I packed her things, and when Noah arrived, she gave me one of her famous, wonderful, long hugs. After she left, my place seemed empty. I found myself missing her more than I thought I would.

The next day, Noah invited me to dinner while Madelyn attended an event at their country club. I would have refused the invitation if Madelyn had been there. On the other hand, if she were home, I am sure I would not have been invited.

After dinner, Noah let me in on a little secret. "We discovered that while she was with you, she never took off any of her underwear. She kept putting the clean ones on over the dirty ones."

"You mean she had three days' worth of underwear on?" I asked.

"Exactly," Noah said, amused.

"I guess I have a lot to learn when it comes to taking care of a little girl," I said.

Noah nodded, laughing.

"Kyra misses Cassie," I said.

"Of course she does."

"So do I."

"You know, Jeff, when I asked for Maddie's hand in marriage, her mother told me, 'If you truly love someone, your love has to last through four seasons.' I never forgot that."

"A wise woman," I said.

"Have you written to Cassie?"

"I have called her every day but haven't written to her, no, sir. I guess letter writing has gone out of style, but I think I'll bring it back," I said.

Noah smiled approvingly.

Later at home I sat down with pen and paper and wrote to Cassie. I told her about my time with Kyra and sent her some pictures of the kids. It was time, and I was ready. I signed the letter *Love you, Jeff.*

A week passed. "I'm coming home," Cassie said in a brief phone call. "Will you pick me up at SeaTac?"

"Of course I will. I love reunions."

I stopped by the Bakers', picked up Kyra, and headed to SeaTac Airport. I was the blond-haired, lily-white, blue-eyed man holding hands with this very black girl. As we walked down the long, polished corridors to Cassie's gate, we left a wake of turned heads and stares. I had to fight the tendency to fall back into my old ways of thinking.

"Look, Daddy! Mommy's here!"

Kyra grabbed my hand and led me toward Cassie.

"Come here, my girl," Cassie said.

Kyra let go of my hand and ran toward Cassie. "Mommy, I missed you so much!"

"So did I," I said.

Cassie was home. My world was complete again. I wrapped my arm around Cassie's tiny waist. We walked through the terminal to the baggage claim area with Kyra holding Cassie's hand. If anyone stared at us, I didn't notice. I had all I needed again. Nothing else mattered. It was that simple.

On Friday night at dinner, Cassie sat close beside me, with some part of her touching me the entire time we were at the restaurant.

"I want to apologize for taking Mom's side against you on Father's Day. I was wrong, and I regret what I did," Cassie said.

"And I apologize for calling your mother a bitch. It will never happen again. You have my word," I said.

"One thing concerns me," Cassie said. "If we start seeing each other all the time again, Mom will push you even harder."

"I thought about that too, but together we will deal with it."

"Nothing will separate us again, Jeff. Not if I have anything to say about it."

It was easy between us again.

The next week, I was busy entertaining out-of-town clients, but Cassie and I managed to work around that and reestablished the old routine of calling each other at bedtime to tuck each other in.

Again, love notes appeared in my truck, and roses showed up on Cassie's desk at work. Good times had come again. We grew closer and stronger each day, at least for a while.

I had put out of my mind that Cassie's past was lying in wait, ready to jump out of the dark and sink its teeth into me.

Chapter 25

It began with a phone call at 10:30 a.m., Friday morning on October 5, 1990. "We need to talk," Cassie said.

"Should I be worried? From the tone of your voice, it sounds serious. Are you all right?"

"No."

"Will I be okay after we have had this talk?"

"No, probably not."

"Cassie, seriously, what's wrong?" I asked, fear creeping up my spine and into my throat.

"Please, Jeff, no more questions. Just meet me at the bar across from my work as soon as you can."

"How about five thirty? We could have dinner afterward."

"You may not want to." Her voice broke slightly.

"See you right after work," I said.

She hung up without saying good-bye. I felt her withdrawal from me, and it scared me.

While I worked, all sorts of scenarios played out in my head, none of them good. Fear squeezed me tightly. It was a long, claustrophobic day, and by the time it was over, I was ready to hear what Cassie had to say, no matter what.

She was waiting for me in the parking lot, looking dead tired and serious. I leaned in to kiss her hello, but she moved her face away from me, averted her gaze, turned, and walked into the bar. I followed as if she were leading me to a slaughterhouse.

We were approaching the one-year mark in our relationship. We had been through so much already. I was convinced that we could handle anything together. That was the deal between us, and until now, I thought it was working.

We sat at the end of the bar. I ordered Baileys. Cassie declined a glass of wine and asked for water instead. Her skin was pale. There were dark circles under her eyes. Her face was clean, without makeup, and her eyelids were puffy. Still, she was beautiful. It was impossible for me not to see beauty when I looked at her, no matter what the circumstances. I fought the urge to kiss her eyelids, to hold her in my arms and tell her that I loved her no matter what.

Two middle-aged men in wrinkled white shirts with open collars and loosened ties sat at the opposite end of the bar, drinking beer and talking sports with the bartender. A small TV on the wall behind the bartender was on an ESPN channel with the volume turned down. Other than that, the bar was empty.

Cassie lit a cigarette. I ordered another Baileys.

"There's no easy way to get into this," she said.

"How about starting at the beginning?" I suggested with one eyebrow raised and, frankly, a little more levity than I had intended.

She inhaled deeply, turning the tip of her cigarette red, burned the tobacco rapidly, and exhaled smoke through her nostrils. Finally, she looked at me with sad but determined eyes and blurted, "I was a phone operator for an out-call service."

"What is an out-call service?"

"It means a prostitute that goes to a client's house. That's what it's called, an out-call service. When they come to the prostitute at the massage parlor, it's an in-call."

"You mean you worked for … a whorehouse?"

She looked me sharply and then reluctantly nodded.

A shockwave ripped through me. My mind raced faster than I could think, bludgeoning me with rearranged images of the woman I loved.

"A friend told me about the opening," she continued.

"But your family had money."

"I had my reasons for doing what I did. That's all I want to say about it."

"Whom did you work for?"

"Frank and Vinny Colacurcio."

"The Mob family? You worked for the Mob?"

"It was just a job, a way to make good money fast."

No amount of bracing could have prevented the incomprehensible explosion of feelings that went off inside me. I took a deep breath and pushed the ball of fire in my belly way down deep. I would deal with it later when I was alone.

I remembered seeing a sign above a strip club in Lake City that said, "We have 100 beautiful and three ugly ones." Rumor had it that Frank Colacurcio owned the place. Colacurcio was one of the leading Mafia bosses in the city, and as a former law-enforcement officer, I knew more than I cared to know about the man and his so-called business.

"There's more," she said. "I am a drug addict."

It was my turn to look down. How could she? What happened to the good Catholic girl, the devoted mother? Had she been acting all along? The part of me that Hazel raised screamed *You idiot!*

I continued to hide my shock and disgust. I let my experience in military intelligence take over. Cassie would see my impenetrable blue eyes and stoic face, no matter what she continued to reveal about her past.

"I'd like to finish this, Jeff. I want you to hear everything. It's time you know it all."

"Go ahead; I won't interrupt."

"I worked for the Colacurcios some time ago, but I quit that job. I'm sober now, and I'm in Alcoholics Anonymous and Narcotics Anonymous. I go to AA and NA meetings regularly."

I thought of New Year's Eve at the Space Needle and Cassie drinking to the point of passing out. I learned later that when she said, "I'm a drug addict," that it was some sort of opening sentence they used at their meetings. At that time, I knew almost nothing about either group.

"Wait—hold on a sec, Cassie," I said.

I glanced at the bartender and the two men. God help me, I wanted to protect Cassie, even at that moment.

"Let's get out of here and find someplace where no one can overhear," I whispered.

"My place?"

"No!" I said a little too sharply and quickly.

"Then where?" she said, attempting to hold back her tears.

"I have an idea."

I led Cassie to my car. It was after six in the evening, and the sun was slightly above the western horizon as we drove down Interstate 90 toward the ferry dock in downtown Seattle. It was one of the last days of Indian summer. We drove straight into the vivid sky over Puget Sound at the peak of sunset, when the colors were most intense and so indescribably beautiful that the boundaries between the heartache I felt and the beauty I saw disappeared, and I wanted to cry.

Cassie must have sensed what I was feeling, because she was the one who burst into tears. The news of her past kept me from reaching for her hand. I would not betray the future for one of us simply because I needed to touch her, to feel comforted in a moment of agonizing beauty.

We walked onto the passenger loading dock with the other pedestrians. The silver water of the sound against the pewter sky drained the color out of us, but it comforted me.

Sea and sky had joined us on our somber journey, like a couple of old friends who loved us unconditionally.

The loudspeaker bellowed, "Last call to Bremerton, Washington. All aboard!"

The ferry workers pushed away from the dock after the all-clear horn sounded. We walked upstairs to the second level. Lining the inner deck port and starboard, large insulated glass windows looked out over the sound and beyond to the Olympic Mountains. Beneath the windows were rows of sparsely populated tables with benches covered in drab brown vinyl. After stopping for coffee at the canteen, I led Cassie to a table in an unoccupied corner.

We sat opposite each other. Being on the water again calmed me, as it had throughout my life. I slowly sipped my coffee and waited patiently.

Cassie's mood remained focused and determined. She began the story of her vertiginous past again. Six hours later, having traveled three times back and forth between Seattle and Bremerton without getting off the ferry, it was over, and all I could think about was getting back on the ground and into the reality of the present.

Chapter 26

Cassie's story slowly bled out of her.

"I was nineteen years old and a sophomore at the University of Washington, living at home and silently resenting my parents for not letting me live on campus. I was sick of Mom's hardnosed rules and Dad's inability to stand up to her on my behalf, but my Catholic upbringing kept me from actually lashing out at her.

"I snuck out at night, after Mom went to bed, to party with my friends. The more I partied, the more I felt stifled at home, and the more I rebelled.

"I heard about an opportunity to make some fast money at an out-call service. The hours were flexible, and the money would buy me a ticket to the freedom I craved. I took the job, no questions asked. After a few days of work, I learned that I was working for the Mafia.

"I worked at the service off and on all the way through college. In my spare time, I hung out with friends from work, one of which was Sheila, a tall, exotic beauty who could walk like a fashion model and swear like a sailor. She had been on her own since she was thirteen, when her parents split up.

"In 1980, I was twenty-three and had my college diploma but with a low overall grade-point average. I soon discovered that good jobs in my chosen field were out of my reach.

"Against Mom and Dad's protests, Sheila and I decided to move to Anchorage, Alaska, with some of her friends. My parents had no idea that Sheila's friends were former strippers and at a club downtown owned by the Colacurcio family.

"It was difficult in the beginning. While our friends were making decent money stripping two or three nights a week, Sheila and I were working twelve-hour days as servers at a local diner. At the end of our first month in Anchorage, we literally had to break open the communal piggy bank to buy a loaf of bread and a jar of pimento cheese to get us through until the next paycheck.

"It was Sheila's idea to learn how to strip, though, honestly I was already thinking about it when she brought it up. We took lessons from our friends, and within a month, we were the new strippers at our friends' club.

"Stripping was fun after I got over the shock of dancing naked in front of strangers. It kept my body in great shape, and the wad of money tucked under my garter belt grew as nights passed and my dancing skills improved.

"One night, a regular customer introduced me to a man named Charlie Mullins. He was handsome, in a Mick Jagger sort of way. He was funny, charming, and seemed interested in me. We began hanging out together. He was a good listener. Everybody knew him, and he was wildly popular at the club.

Women threw themselves at him, but he wanted me. In a couple of weeks, we became obsessed with each other. I know it sounds crazy, but in my young mind, I mistook obsession for love. That was really when the trouble started for me.

"Charlie was always front and center stage at the club and when I was with him. I felt like a celebrity. Although I didn't realize it at the time, the fact that he was black and thus taboo made me love him more.

"I was happy, at first. Charlie was skilled and tender in bed. He taught me how to let go and give in to the pleasures my body could give me. With Charlie's love and attention, my self-esteem soared, and for the first time in my life, I felt powerful and secure.

"When I moved in with Charlie, I decided not to leave a forwarding address for my parents. Charlie was my family now. I would do anything for him, and I was sure he felt the same way about me. How terribly naïve I was.

"Sheila was the one who broke the truth about Charlie to me. She said, 'Cassie, honey, listen to me. Some of the old-timers at the club swear that Charlie's a pimp.'

"'Prove it,' I said to her.

"She said, okay, if that's what it took. She would show me proof. She drove a few miles east of the club and turned on to a street lined with old-growth conifers and elegant houses run down by urban decay.

"Sheila pulled into the driveway of a two-story townhouse. The roof sagged from heavy winters. Sweat trickled down the windows along the front of the house. Heavily stained curtains hung in disarray, leaving peepholes of light for passersby who were brave enough to step up close and look inside.

"Sheila drove me around back and parked her car. She led me to the back-door entrance and pressed the back doorbell. A female voice said. 'Can I help you?'

"Sheila asked if Charlie was there, and the voice said, 'Who wants to know?' Then Sheila said something in French, and the door opened. I asked her what the French words meant, and she said she didn't know, just that she was told it was the password to get in.

"A top-heavy, middle-aged woman with badly damaged short blonde hair opened the door and invited us inside. She looked at Sheila as if she recognized her. I asked Sheila if she had been there before and she said yes, once.

"We followed the woman down the long, narrow hallway and into a sitting room lined with tattered Victorian loveseats. Large prints of naked cherubs in plastic frames hung on faded velvet walls. The woman told us to wait, that Charlie was taking care of some business.

"From somewhere upstairs, Frank Sinatra crooned 'It Was a Very Good Year.' I listened for telltale sounds but couldn't make out anything definite. Still, I knew Sheila was right about Charlie, and I told her so.

"We got up to leave. On our way out, I heard Charlie laughing, his voice trailing down the stairs. A young girl barely out of her teens with pale blue-white skin and gaunt eyes hung on to him as if he were her only source of life. She whispered something to him, and then he kissed her mouth. His fingers touched her see-through blouse and found her stiff nipples. She grinned wickedly.

"I ran out of the back door. Sheila yelled at me to wait up. We ran to the car and sped away.

"I lost it. I wanted to hit somebody. I kept yelling, 'I hate him! I hate him!' Sheila pulled into the parking lot at the club. She grabbed me as I sobbed and held me, rocking me back and forth. She said we had a show to do in less than an hour and that I needed to get it together. She said she was there for me and helped me calm down.

"I walked into the club and sat down at the bar, lit a cigarette, ordered three shots of Jack Daniel's, and gulped them down, one stinging shot after the other. Then I walked into the dressing room and dressed for the show. In a whiskey haze, I pole danced and lap danced and stripped down to nothing but my rage. At some point, I blacked out.

"When I woke up the next morning in Sheila's bed, I found myself covered with cash. Sheila walked in with a pot of coffee, and with a smile, she told me that I broke the record for the most cash ever made by one dancer in a single night at the club.

"I said, 'Whoop-de-doo,' and told her to forget the coffee. I got up, went to the kitchen cabinet, and poured myself a shot of whiskey."

Chapter 27

Cassie pulled a cigarette from her purse and grabbed her Zippo lighter. I helped her slip into her jacket and walked with her out onto the deck. She was lost in the past; I was lost in the present.

The cold wind slapped her cheeks. Her hair lashed at her face like hundreds of cracking whips. She stepped into a pocket of calm air in a protected corner and lit her cigarette, her face pensive and melancholy.

I walked to the stern of the ferry. As familiar as an old romantic postcard, the light of the Seattle Space Needle played on the surface of the black night water. I thought of our midnight dance at the Space Needle on New Year's Eve, and a pang of nostalgia swept through me. Then it was gone forever, replaced by the newer version, tainted with the knowledge of what I now knew.

Cassie stepped beside me, her arms folded tightly across her chest. I took off my jacket and wrapped it around her shoulders. Her body shivered. We walked back inside to our table. Cassie sat down and rubbed her hands together briskly. I brought a fresh round of coffee to the table, and after Cassie warmed up, she continued.

"You would think I would have left Alaska after I learned about Charlie, but frankly, I felt I had no place to go. He hounded me with phone calls and love notes. He left me messages telling me I was the one and only love of his life and that he could explain things if I would just let him. His voice sounded desperate, and I missed him, as crazy as that sounds. I agreed to meet him at the club, and he said and did just the right things to pull me back toward him. Honestly, I wanted to believe his lies, so I tricked myself into believing that things would change for the better.

"I willingly went back to Charlie, and for a while, it was a sweet homecoming. He doled out another round of devotion. He swore he had been and would continue to be faithful to me and that his pimping business was 'just a way to make money,' that what I saw with the girl on the stairs was 'just a game,' a necessary evil, and that it meant nothing to him. He charmed me all over again, and it felt warm and delicious, just like the whiskey shots I downed every night.

"As the months passed, Charlie began to share details of his business with me. He promised to save his money, retire early, marry me, and we would live a life of wealth and leisure, and he wanted to share it all with me.

"What I left back home in Bellevue was my sense of what was right and wrong. The only thing that mattered to me was getting high and being with Charlie. He made sure that I had a limitless supply of alcohol and marijuana, and eventually cocaine.

"I don't remember exactly how it happened; the details are hazy—but Charlie convinced me that I would be doing us both a favor if I started hooking for him. I discussed the idea with Sheila, and she confessed that she'd been hooking for a while.

"It was a natural step, really. My body was a commodity; stripping had taught me that. In my mind and in the minds of my friends, it made sense for us to up the ante and gamble our bodies for pots of gold and the end of our rainbows.

"I did it, Jeff; I became a hooker. Charlie taught me all about what turned men on. The more hooking I did, the better I became at the gymnastics of sex and the calculated well-timed phrases of lust. It was a job, a game, and I was the winner who won the jackpot every time.

"I learned later that if you got caught hooking, it was a class-B misdemeanor in Alaska with a fine up to a couple thousand dollars, and that pimping was a class-B felony, and if Charlie got caught, his fine would be up to a hundred thousand.

"The funny thing is, I never thought about getting caught or being arrested. Nor did I worry about the consequences of a criminal record.

"Business was good. I began to get requests from regular customers, though I didn't get a kick out of it, except that it pleased Charlie. I didn't feel guilty; I felt nothing at all.

"If I started to spiral down, Charlie would pump me up again with promises and later with cocaine, until I was flying high again. The more money I made for Charlie, the sweeter he was to me. I hurled myself headlong into the lifestyle of a hooker. My life in Bellevue was a colorless memory, a dim life that someone else had lived.

"I had unprotected sex with Charlie. Maybe it was wishful thinking on my part, but I trusted him. My everyday life became a continual series of parties that lasted until dawn, hooking, sleeping until noon, and preening myself for the next performance. Then two years later, it all fell apart, leaving me with a spent bond and a bankrupt soul.

"It was the summer of 1985. Afternoons were warm and stretched longer and longer until the sun was in the sky for nearly twenty hours. The long daylight slowed business down, so Charlie decided to kick things up a notch with a vacation. I invited Sheila and my friend from the club, and Charlie invited his people to join us aboard Charlie's new boat, *Euphoria*. We would sail around the Gulf of Alaska and anchor in the Bering Sea for a week, going inland for supplies when needed, and of course, the partying would be nonstop.

"For the first few days, it was a blast. In the afternoons, we found ourselves waking up together on the floor, our arms and legs all tangled up together. We nursed Bloody Marys, sunbathed, slept, then ate and slept again.

"The women whale-watched and painted each other's toenails while the men played poker and smoked cigars. At midnight, the sun finally dropped beneath the sea. Then the hard, wild partying began.

"God only knows how much alcohol and drugs we consumed. We partied until daybreak, when Charlie circulated trays of sleeping pills and tranquilizers for those of us who were still standing. I remember what it was like sleeping aboard the *Euphoria*. It was deep, black sleep, like being under anesthesia before surgery.

"A couple of days before the vacation ended, I felt sick. I thought I had come down with some sort of delayed seasickness or maybe bad hangover, but for whatever reason, Charlie's drug cocktail didn't work anymore. I was so tired that all I wanted to do was curl up in a ball under the sheets and wait for sleep, which never came. The next morning, I forced myself out of bed and threw up on the way to the toilet. The nausea and vomiting stayed with me throughout the day. Food disgusted me, so I didn't eat. I drank instead.

"At some point during the night's festivities, Charlie slipped me an extra line of cocaine. It helped some, but I was dead tired. I gave up and collapsed in the bed before the party was over.

"Charlie woke me up at dawn and scolded me for leaving the party early. I pulled the covers over my head and told him to go away, that I was sick. He yanked the covers off me, grabbed me, and stood me up. I threw up all over him.

"Charlie went into a rage, picked up my suitcase, and threw it at me, knocking me down. Then he grabbed a clean shirt and banged out of the cabin in a fury.

"I had seen Charlie angry with others but never with me. It shocked me, but at the same time, I never felt guilty for not being there for him when he needed me. I pulled myself together and joined the party on the deck. I waded through the crowd and found Sheila.

"She said I looked like shit. I told her what happened with Charlie and she said, 'Don't piss the pimp.'

"I sucked it up, and was the last one standing at the party. Then Charlie and I made up in bed.

"After docking the *Euphoria* at the yacht club in Anchorage, Charlie stayed behind to pay the tabs, and I went home to rest.

"Sheila called as soon as I walked in the door, saying she needed to see me immediately and that it was urgent. Tired and still nauseated, I drove to her apartment. She was standing in the doorway, waiting for me, holding an appointment card. 'Who's that for?' I asked.

"'You need a test,' she said.

"It was positive.

"'Get an abortion,' she said.

"I told her no. It was against my beliefs. I'll never forget what she said next.

"'What beliefs?'

"For the first time since leaving Bellevue, the Catholic girl I once was rose up, stepped away, and observed what I had become. She screamed at me, 'Shame on you!'

"I folded in on myself and felt a strong suicidal urge, but the life inside me kept me from harming myself. After I regained my composure, I went home. Charlie was waiting for me. I told him right away.

"'Great news!' he said, holding me in his arms. I was shocked that he was happy about it.

"Near the end of the first trimester, I was still nauseated and vomiting all day long. I had had enough of hooking, so I told Charlie I wanted to quit.

"'No, sugar, you can't. You have to be strong,' he said.

"'Why?' I asked.

"Because, he said, some men would pay a lot of money to have sex with a pregnant woman and with money coming in faster, we could start over right after the baby was born. We would be a real family. We would move away where there were fewer stigmas against interracial families. My Catholic side calmed down and went back to sleep after hearing that I could go on and deliver the baby and thus redeem myself as a mother."

Chapter 28

"I worried constantly that my more athletic clients would hurt the baby in some way. My breasts hurt, and all I wanted to do was sleep. When I began to show, Charlie saw huge dollar signs, which infuriated me.

"One morning about midway into the pregnancy, I came dragging in at dawn from a particularly grueling night of hooking and was surprised to find Charlie sitting at the kitchen table. When I asked him why he was up so early, he complained that I was bringing in less cash, not scheduling as many appointments and that I was dragging my lazy feet on purpose.

"I fell into a rage. It was the first time I lost my temper with him, and the thing is, it felt good. I think I actually scared him, because he stood up and backed away from me and then left the house.

"We argued all the time after that, and each time he stormed out. At first, it was for an hour or two, but with each fight, he stayed gone longer. By the time I was in my third trimester, he would leave and not come home for days, but then he would show up and act like nothing happened.

"It seemed that Sheila was backing away from me too, though I couldn't pinpoint anything specific. When I asked her what was wrong, she would say, 'Oh nothing, honey, everything's fine, you're just real sensitive because of the baby and all.'

"I tried hard not to think about my swelling belly and concentrated on making more money for Charlie so he would come back to me and we could continue our plan for the future. In January, when the darkness stretched seventeen hours, I worked double shifts. The stack of hundred-dollar bills on the dresser got so tall that it toppled over, much to Charlie's delight. Sure enough, he came back to our bed.

"When I got home from work in the predawn hours of April 3, 1995, the house was empty. I crawled into bed and waited for my body to give in to the hounding fatigue that had consumed me for months. A couple of hours later, I waddled to the bathroom to pee. Warm, blood-tinged liquid streamed down my legs and soaked my socks.

"I had no idea where Charlie was, so I called Sheila. She drove me to Alaska Regional Hospital emergency room and left me sitting in a wheelchair with an emergency room nurse standing beside me. She promised to find Charlie and bring him back with her.

"The nurse frowned when I told her I had not had any prenatal care, not even a prenatal vitamin, had no insurance and very little cash with me. She wheeled me inside, and after a brief examination, the emergency room doctor admitted me to the maternity ward as a charity case.

"The pain came in waves. I was scared out of my mind, and it hurt so much that I could barely breathe. I closed my eyes to be alone with the pain.

"Hours later, my bed jerked. I heard a voice saying, 'Call the doctor; she's ready.' They moved my bed down the hall into a brightly light room that smelled of alcohol. Gloved hands fell in and out of my view. A sheet flew over me. Suddenly, I felt the need to bear down.

"'Push!' the nurse yelled.

"Someone grabbed my hand, and then I heard Sheila's voice cheering me on. I pushed hard for what seemed like a long time, even though it hurt and I was beyond exhaustion. Then I felt arms pulling me up, and a few seconds later, someone said, 'It's a girl.'

"They laid me back down, and I heard her cry. The nurse placed her on my chest. She was warm and light as a feather. There was a lot of curly black hair. Her skin was the color of caramel candy. Her fingers were pink and tiny. She had a perfect mouth. Her lips made a little o as she turned her face toward me. She was so pure that it made me cry.

"I didn't know how I was going to do it, and I know I had a long way to go to become the mother I needed to be, but the job was mine and mine only. I would find a way. They took the baby away so I could rest. When I woke up, Sheila was gone. Charlie never showed up, nor did he come to the new daddy's dinner the next evening.

"The next morning, I filled out of the necessary paperwork, including the form for the birth certificate, and wrote her name for the first time: Kyra Dawn Mullins.

"I called a cab and took Kyra home to meet her father. I was surprised to find the front door unlocked. I walked in, placed my sleeping baby and the gift sack of diapers and formula on the couch and called out, 'Charlie?'

"Music was coming from the bedroom. I remember thinking that Charlie must have gone to sleep with it still playing. Unlike me, he could sleep through a hurricane. I tiptoed down the hall, turned the doorknob, and stepped inside. The blackout curtains were drawn. The room was pitch-black. I waited for my eyes to adjust to the dark.

"The room smelled of dank, dirty linens and a mixture of stale cigarettes and pot. They were heaving together, grunting and moaning, and the head of the bed was pounding against the wall. Shadows came into focus. Charlie lay in the bed faceup watching Sheila riding him, her breasts bouncing wildly in the air, her sweating skin slapping against his.

"I threw whatever I could grab at them. Sitting in a plastic tray on the top of the chest of drawers was a large, partially eroded mound of cocaine. I threw fistfuls of the white powder at them, then picked up the tray and threw the whole mound of snow on top of them, along with the tray. Light flooded the room. Sheila was out of bed, her hands on the light switch. She screamed and ran out of the room.

"Charlie lunged at me, but he was drunk and high. I tried to jump out of his way, but he grabbed me and threw me against the wall. He held me down and rammed his fist in my face repeatedly. I felt the stamp of his heavy gold ring as it crashed against my forehead and my nose. My mouth filled with blood faster than I could spit it out.

"The baby began to cry. Charlie hesitated. He must have heard her too. I made a move to get away, and he came at me again with his fist, hard. My nose popped and went numb. I reached up to protect my face with my hands, but it was too late. My front teeth were missing. My tongue found them lodged on the inside of my lower lip.

"Grabbing the nearest bedpost, I pulled myself up off the floor and stumbled into the hallway. I heard Charlie fall against the bedroom door and ran as fast as I could to the kitchen, found the keys to Charlie's car, grabbed the baby and the supplies from the hospital, ran to the car, and locked the baby and me inside. The car keys slipped out of my bloody hands onto the floor. I ripped into the box of Pampers and wiped my hands as best I could with one.

"While I ducked under the steering wheel to find the keys, the back door opened at the same time my right hand touched Charlie's Playboy rabbit foot keychain. In a panic, I fumbled, found the ignition key, started the car, backed up, turned around, dodged Charlie, and rammed the gas pedal to the floor. I shot out of the driveway. Gravel flew everywhere, and I drove as far away as I could. On the outskirts of town, I saw a phone booth next to a drive-by coffee stand; I pulled over and dialed out the only number I could think of. Thank the holy mother of God, he answered.

"'Frank, it's me,' I said. 'The baby and me—we need help.'"

Chapter 29

"I met Frank at a hookup. He was a lonely, old widower who would call for an appointment. We would talk and do nothing else, and he would pay me the full price every time. We gradually became friends. When I had time, I would stop by his place with a bucket of Kentucky Fried Chicken, biscuits, and coleslaw. The man was a Kentucky Fried Chicken fanatic.

"Frank picked us up and drove us to the hospital that had discharged us earlier that day. The same emergency room nurse examined me, cleaned me up, and gave me some Tylenol and an ice pack for my nose. She asked if I wanted to press charges, but I declined. Frank paid the emergency room bill and took us home with him. On the way there, he talked me into doing what I dreaded most: calling my parents.

"Mom answered. I heard myself telling her that I had fallen in love with a pimp, slept with him, lived with him, hooked for him, had his baby, and after he broke my nose and knocked out my teeth, I stole his car and barely escaped with my life and baby. I told her like it had happened to some other Cassie, not me, and I was the tattletale.

"I waited for Mom to scold me or say, 'I told you so' or 'You made your bed, now lay in it,' but she didn't. What she said was, 'What are you going to do?'

"'Please, Mom, can I come home with the baby for a while?' I asked.

"'If you come home it will be on my terms,' she said.

"I promised her that I would obey her, and with her help I would turn my life around and learn to be a good mother to Kyra.

"Frank gave me the money for a plane ticket back home. The last thing he said to me as we boarded the plane for Seattle was, 'Good luck starting over, and whatever you do, don't come back here.'

"Mom and Dad were at the gate waiting for me when we landed in Seattle. They were horrified when they got a good look at my injuries.

"Mom took the baby, looked at her black face briefly, and with a look of embarrassment, handed her back to me, saying, 'You should have told us she was black.'

"I became Mom's new mission.

"'You'll do whatever I tell you, when I tell you, how I tell you,' she said.

"'You have my word,' I said.

"When I walked in the door at home, the new nanny that Mom hired took Kyra away from me, fed her, bathed her, and rocked her to sleep.

"'Don't unpack,' Mom said. Dad drove me to the Overlake Hospital and had me admitted. Over the next several weeks, various specialists fixed my nose, my teeth, and my cheekbone. My injuries slowly healed, but I was still secretly suffering from alcoholism and drug addiction. The doctors sent me home on strong pain medication, and when the pills ran out, I was desperate for a high.

"After Mom and Dad went to bed, I started sneaking into their bedroom and stealing cash. Then I would crawl out of my bedroom window, as I had done so many times in high school, and get high with druggie friends from college. There I was again, comfortably leading a secret life. I had lived this way for so long that the thought never entered my mind that it was wrong, that I was betraying myself as well as my parents.

"Kyra was the one who forced me to come clean. It still hurts to think about what might have happened to her on my watch. She was eight months old, active and crawling everywhere. It was early morning, and I was hung over from partying the night before.

"Instead of putting Kyra in her baby bed, I let her crawl around on the floor while I took a long, hot shower. Dripping wet, I stepped into the bedroom, toweled off, and sat down at the dresser, absentmindedly combing the tangles out of my hair. It was quiet in the room. Kyra was missing.

"I ran down the hall, calling for her, searching everywhere for her. She was too young to hide from me. I ran back to the bedroom to look again and noticed that one of the full-length windows that opened at the bottom was ajar from the previous night's outing. Kyra was missing, and it was my fault. I started shaking, crying uncontrollably. What kind of mother was I? I calmed down just enough to call 911. A few minutes later, two police officers rang the front doorbell. I grabbed my house robe and answered the door, shaking violently, on the verge of hyperventilating. I led them to the bedroom and pointed to the open window, then followed them outside and sat down on the front steps crying uncontrollably while they combed the neighborhood, looking for Kyra.

"An hour later, they were still looking. Mom drove up and saw me crying on the front steps, with nothing on but a cotton robe. The two police cars, their lights flashing, were blocking the driveway. She ran up the sidewalk and screamed, 'Get inside the house now!'

"'Mom, Kyra is missing, and it's my fault,' I cried.

"In a moment of vulnerability and self-hatred, I confessed what I had done, that I was still on drugs, stole from her on a regular basis, snuck out at night to party, left the window open, and Kyra crawled away.

"'You promised!' she screamed.

"One of the police officers interrupted us, carrying Kyra in his arms. She had been missing for more than an hour. He found her five houses away, crawling under some large bushes. She was dirty and scratched up but was okay otherwise, he said.

"Mom told me to take Kyra and clean her up while she talked to the police officers. After they left, she called a friend to watch Kyra. Without a word of explanation, she drove me to Fairfax Psychiatric Hospital and left me at the front desk. I went through detoxification and a whole lot more.

"Six months later, I left the hospital clean and sober. They released me back to Mom's care, with strict instructions to attend ninety twelve-step meetings in ninety days or I would risk losing custody of my daughter.

"I continued to maintain my sobriety and went to meetings regularly. I got a job at Sears, worked there for a few months, and then took my present job because it paid slightly more and the hours were better. I had just celebrated twelve months of sobriety when I met you that day in the park."

"When did you start drinking again?" I asked.

"I gradually began drinking a glass of white wine, limiting myself to no more than two after we met."

"Except for the New Year's Eve party," I said.

"Oh, that. Yes, I was nervous and fell off the wagon that night. The next day, I went to an AA meeting, which helped me get back on track. Sobriety is a one-day-at-a-time kind of thing, Jeff, and for the most part, my recovery time continues in the right direction."

The Seattle skyline came into view for the last time. The ferry closed for the evening after it docked. It felt good to be on dry land again. I drove Cassie back to her car. We were both too exhausted and emotionally drained to speak. She paused before she got in her car and looked into my eyes the way she did when we first met.

"Is there anything else?" I asked.

"No, it's just that, well, I'm truly sorry that it took me so long to tell you."

"Me too," I said.

"It's true what they say that we are as sick as our secrets," she said as tears streamed down her face. "And I didn't want to be sick anymore."

In that moment, I saw the real Cassie as she blinked her tears away, her face full of relief, her sad, vulnerable eyes letting me in all the way, no matter the consequences. I realized the truth about her: she had become very brave and strong.

Chapter 30

I camped out at the office after work. What I needed was a good road trip by myself, so I scheduled back-to-back out-of-town business trips through the end of October. Abbey was the only person who knew where I was going and for how long. At lunch the week before I left town, Abbey sipped her coffee and toyed with her food.

"You're unusually quiet today," I said. "What gives?"

"I'm waiting for you to tell me what's wrong," she said.

"It's nothing to worry about. I'm crazy busy at work and have a lot on my mind."

"How long have we known each other?" she said.

"Long enough," I said, raising an eyebrow.

"That's exactly my point, Jeff. I know you. Work is not what is eating at you."

"I don't want to talk about it."

"Are you getting cold feet? Is that it?"

"Look, Abbey, I just need to get away for a while, okay?"

"Now I'm really worried," she said.

"I'm serious. Back off. Now's not a good time."

"Whoa," she said, looking a little hurt. "Okay, stranger."

Abbey, as usual, was right. I had become a stranger, not only to her but also to myself. Being on the road among other strangers comforted me. While away, I checked my answering machine for work-related messages and erased the rest without listening to them. At night when I lay awake, I got up and wrote in my journal until sleep came.

I called the boys every night at their bedtime and checked in with Abbey once a week. My few phone calls to Cassie were brief, light, and superficial.

The road trip uncluttered my life and calmed me down. Gradually my mind cleared, and I regained the ability to focus on the present. I spent time pinpointing my conflicting feelings for Cassie. I still loved her and felt fierce loyalty to her, especially in light of her confessions to me. She clearly loved Kyra, as did I. I could see us working well together as partners and as a family unit with Kyra and the boys. However, I was not entirely convinced that she could maintain her sobriety for the long term. Her unpredictable mood swings and rebellious, secretive nature scared me. I had to face the fact that she could lapse back into her old ways and destroy the family we were working hard to create.

It was time to go home again, and I was ready to stop the rhetoric in my head and start living again. Cassie was good for me that way. She got me out of my head and into the real world of the living, with all its messy loose ends.

The first weekend back home fell on Halloween, so Cassie and I took the kids trick-or-treating. Kyra wore a devil costume and acted like one too. She refused to trick-or-treat with Cassie and the boys and wanted me all to herself.

By the end of the evening, all three kids were on a major sugar high. The boys eventually calmed down, but Kyra stubbornly resisted our efforts to get her to go to bed. It was an exhausting evening, and I was relieved when it was time to go home.

Despite Kyra's bed behavior, Cassie and I easily fell back into our previous routine. We met for happy hour at Black Angus three to four times a week and kept in touch continuously over the phone. Cassie never wanted to talk about her past again, not even with me, and I complied with her wishes. We simply moved on. I looked forward to smooth waters and clear skies for a while. Indeed, things seemed back to normal between us, even better than normal. Then we found ourselves in stormy waters again.

It was a cold November morning, and the weatherman was predicting heavy snowfall by the end of the day. Unfortunately, Kyra left her wool hat and gloves at home, so I volunteered to stop by Cassie's place, pick them up, and take them to Kyra on my way to work.

On the kitchen table, an official-looking letter lay open on top of a stack of Christmas catalogs and advertisement circulars. I glanced briefly at it and noticed a letterhead. It was from the Internal Revenue Service. A stamp in big red letters read "FINAL NOTICE" in the empty space between the date and the address line of the letter.

Reading someone's private mail was not on my list of personal vices, but this was not just someone. With Cassie's recent confessions, I was not about to leave her apartment without reading what was in that letter. Anything that affected her also affected me—or at least that was my excuse for reading it.

Cassie owed the IRS $160,000. I called her at work and asked her to meet me for an urgent lunch.

"I thought you told me everything," I said, throwing the letter down in front of her.

"So you're reading my mail now," she said sharply. "Is that how it's going to be with us from now on?"

"That's entirely up to you. You were the one who said there would be no more secrets."

"I didn't tell you because I didn't want you to get tangled up in more fallout from my past."

"Don't try to protect me, Cassie. I can take care of myself. Just tell me what this is about."

"It's about the time I worked for the Colacurcio family," she said.

"For the out-call service," I said.

"Right," she said. "They paid my salary in cash, no taxes withheld. It was all under the table."

"Not paying taxes didn't concern you, even a little?" I asked.

"I didn't think about it, Jeff. It was another stupid mistake in a long line of mistakes and errors in judgment I made at the time. I am ashamed to admit it now, but back then, I was actually dumb enough to believe I'd never get caught. And it gets worse, Jeff. When I moved to Alaska, I forgot about the whole thing."

"Apparently, the IRS didn't forget," I said.

"This past summer, after we broke up, I had heard through the grapevine that the Colacurcio family had been indicted for tax fraud. The rumor was that my bosses owned and operated a whole string of strip clubs and that the government was investigating allegations of unreported income from the clubs in Washington and in Alaska."

"Alaska? Is this another secret? Did the Colacurcio family own the club where you worked? Was Charlie's business part of their business?"

"Like I said, there was a lot of gossip going around. I wouldn't vouch for it even if I could, and I can't. It may be coincidental, but I received the first letter from the IRS about the back taxes I owed a couple of weeks after I heard the news about the indictment."

"Who knows about these letters?" I asked.

"Nobody, and I want it to stay that way," she said. "A few weeks later, the IRS sent out a second warning letter saying that the longer I delayed the payment, the more interest and penalties I owed."

"A hundred and sixty grand is a lot of money. The numbers don't add up, Cassie. The only way you could accrue this much tax debt ..."

"Is if I never reported a red cent to the IRS the whole time I was stripping and was hooking," she said.

"Shit," I said, shaking my head.

"The final notice letter came this morning, demanding that I pay something toward the balance immediately," she said.

"What are you going to do?"

"You know I don't have that kind of money, but at the same time, I don't want my parents to know about this. I was sitting here trying to come up with some kind of payment plan when you called."

"Let me see what I can do," I said.

"No."

"I still have some connections. I could poke around and see what comes up."

"Now do you see why I didn't tell you about this?" she sighed. "I knew you would risk your own reputation for my sake."

"What reputation?" I grinned, and she smiled faintly.

"Why do you want to do this for me after all the trouble I have caused you?" she said as she looked down at her hands.

I walked around the table and sat down beside her, pulling her chin up, tilting her face so she would look at me. She continued to look down, too ashamed to look at me.

"Because," I said, taking her hands in mine and kissing them gently, "I love you."

Chapter 31

It was a well-kept secret that Internal Revenue Service employees like Mimi Stuart worked in incognito offices across the country. The particular location had a FedEx counter downstairs that disguised Mimi's IRS office upstairs. I knew Mimi from my old days working for the Washington State Patrol. Mimi's official title was fiscal accountant. She worked twenty-four-hour shifts every other day, during which she was available to the IRS authorities at a moment's notice, even if it was in the middle of the night. When her pager went off, she would stop what she was doing, drive immediately to the scene of the crime, physically count the cash, apprehend and record it in the IRS databanks.

"Well, well, if it isn't Officer Green," Mimi said, getting up to shake my hand as I approached her desk.

"Just Jeff." I smiled. "It's been awhile. How's the Mafia's worst nightmare come true doing?"

"Meaner than ever, so you better watch yourself, Jeff. Pull up a chair and tell me how the heck you are."

We kicked around some old stories from when we worked together, and we caught each other up briefly on our lives.

"I'm sure you didn't come here just to reminisce," she said, peering at me over her reading glasses. "What can I do for you?"

"I need your help if you're willing. Let me buy you some lunch, and I'll fill you in on the details."

"Buy me lunch, and I'm putty in your hands," she said with a laugh. I remembered how Mimi could eat anybody under the table. Lucky for her, she also had the body of a linebacker, since her job required that she frequent some of Seattle's highest-crime areas.

We ate at Daniel's Broiler, one of the best steakhouses on the east side, and gorged on juicy New York strips with all the fixings. Over dessert, I told her about Cassie and her IRS problem.

"Your girlfriend's tax file is not personally handled by me, but I'll make some inquiries and see what I can find out," she said.

The next morning, she called. "I have Cassie's file sitting on my desk right now."

"I'll be right over."

Twenty minutes later, I was in her office, thanking her for the quick response.

"Here's what I can do for you," she said. "Fifty thousand will make this go away entirely; no questions asked, no further inquiries, nothing."

"Much obliged, Mimi. Anytime you're in the mood for Daniel's, I'm your man."

"You've gone and done it now," she bellowed as I walked toward the stairs. "Next week. Same time, same place."

"See you then. Don't be late," I said, knowing she would take me up on the offer.

Unfortunately, it was during this time that my cash flow situation was a bit pinched. I could come up with $32,000 cash, but it would take some time to liquidate more of my assets. I thought about the possible quick solution and decided to take a calculated risk.

When Cassie and I got back together, Noah invited me to the country club to play golf with him. Since golf was not all that much fun to me, I managed to come up with some valid excuses to decline. However, I had a good reason to take him up on his next golf invitation.

Despite my agreeing not to discuss her tax problems with her family, I felt it was in Cassie's best interest to break my promise to her. Noah and I needed to talk man to man about her situation. The golf invitation came, and I accepted. We were on the last hole of the front nine, walking down to the green, when I told Noah about Cassie's letter from the IRS.

"I thought you'd want to know, even though I promised Cassie I wouldn't tell you."

Noah rubbed his chin, took his golf hat off, scratched his head, cleaned his glasses, and paced nervously back and forth until the golfers behind us yelled for us to move on.

"I need to think about this, Jeff, though I know there isn't much time. If you don't mind, I'd like to discuss the matter with Mitchell and see what our options are legally."

"Sure, of course, as long as Madelyn is kept out of the loop. Cassie would freak out if Madelyn got wind of this."

"You have my word," he said.

I regretted telling Noah as soon as the words came out of my mouth. When I got home, there was a message on the machine.

"Jeff, it's Mitchell. Dad just called me and told me about Cassie. He wants you to call him right away."

I immediately called Noah.

"I want to write a check for the entire fifty grand," Noah said.

"You're going to write a check that size and not tell Madelyn?" I said nervously. "Won't she be suspicious when the check comes through your bank statement?"

"Perhaps—well, yes," he said.

"Just write a check for eighteen," I said. "I'll take care of the rest. This will put the whole thing to bed. You could tell Madelyn that you're investing in a new project I've got going."

"I'm not sure Maddie will buy that idea, but it's worth a try. We'll do it your way," he said hesitantly.

"Just make the check out to my company name," I added.

"I'll mail it today," he said. "But under ordinary circumstances, I don't keep things from my wife. I hope you understand that."

He was going to tell her. I knew it as soon as we hung up. A few days later, Mitchell called, saying that Noah gave in and told Madelyn about the IRS situation after she had seen the check and interrogated him about it.

That afternoon, I handed Mimi a check for fifty grand. She wrote out a receipt and handed it to me with her best wishes. I picked Cassie up after work and took her to a restaurant on Lake Washington. I handed her the envelope with the receipt in it and waited for her reaction.

"You didn't."

"I did." I told her about my meetings with Mimi, but I left out the part about Noah's contribution.

"How did you come up with that kind of money?" she asked.

"I borrowed it," I lied and quickly changed the subject.

Three days later, Cassie called me at work.

"Where did you get the money, Jeff?" she asked angrily.

"I told you, I borrowed it."

"You're lying. You got the money from my folks."

"It was mostly my money. Your dad paid a part of it, yes. Who told you?"

"Never mind who told me. I thought I could trust you."

She hung up. So much for me thinking I was being smart about this. Noah called me soon after and confessed to me that he had told Madelyn. "Maddie promised that she wouldn't let on that she knew."

"I broke Cassie's promise, you broke mine, and Madelyn broke yours—lesson learned."

"I'm sorry, Jeff, but I wanted to let you know that Cassie is on the warpath."

"We'll work it out," I said.

"That could be difficult," Noah said. "She's not speaking to you."

Despite Noah's warning that Cassie had cut me off again, I was sure that things would smooth over, and that is exactly what happened after a few days of the silent treatment. There was no stopping us.

By the middle of November, we were back to the business of being together again. There was also a new routine in our life as a couple: Sunday dinner at the Bakers', where Madelyn and I fine-tuned our skills at avoiding each other.

We had beaten the odds. We entered a period of sustainable happiness. Sleepovers were frequent. It was me usually staying at Cassie's place. My life consisted of work and Cassie. Again, I neglected other parts of my life. I put off calling Abbey and Clint, thinking I would call later, only later never came. My life was too full to notice that the outside world had again vanished.

Cassie and I became the partners I had envisioned while on my road trip. Kyra's temper tantrums slowly improved as our family solidified. We were hopeful for the future, and it seemed the worst was behind us.

The Saturday after Thanksgiving, Abbey invited the boys, Kyra, Cassie, and me for a delayed celebration. The kids got along famously, especially Stacey and Kyra. As we were about to leave, Abbey asked if Kyra could come to Stacey's sleepover the next weekend. We jumped at the chance, and on the way home, Cassie and I planned our own sleepover in the mountains.

About forty miles from Yakima, Washington, nestled in the Cascade Mountains along highway 410, was an old mountain lodge at Chinook Pass called Whistling Jack's. My favorite cabin, the one named The Grandview, was situated right on the Naches River, with a hot tub on the deck overlooking the river. The view from the hot tub on a clear winter's night was the closest thing to heaven on earth for me, and I wanted to share it with Cassie.

On Friday, November 30, Cassie and I dropped Kyra off at Abbey's for the weekend. I rented a four-wheel-drive truck and hauled snowmobiles on the trailer in back. Cassie had never been on a snowmobile, nor had she skied, and she was a bit nervous.

We arrived at Whistling Jack's in time to freshen up and dress for dinner. Afterward, we went back to the cabin and played in the hot tub. Cassie glowed in the silver moonlight. A mist halo surrounded her, and her skin shimmered with thousands of tiny diamonds. I thought I was seeing a beautiful mirage. Not in my wildest fantasies could I have imagined this moment. I memorized the shape of her body in the water, the exact positions of the moon and the stars, and the sound of the river current as it crashed against the rocks below.

She slowly slid under the water up to her eyes, her long, dark hair spread out in a half moon on the surface. Her toes softly, playfully touched between my legs. I responded immediately. She giggled and disappeared under the water.

I closed my eyes as she came close to me. I tried to grab her and pull her into my arms, but it was like trying to catch a fish with bare hands. She slithered underneath me, swimming in and out under my legs. It drove me crazy with desire. With my eyes still closed, I ducked under the water. Suddenly her mouth was on mine, her long hair swirling around me like warm seaweed. I had to have her.

I opened my eyes underwater. She had slipped out of her bikini. Tiny silver bubbles covered her illuminated turquoise body as she passed underneath my legs again. I pulled her up and out of the water and carried her into the cabin. We fell on the bear rug in front of the fire without drying off.

Hours later, we curled up together and went to sleep like contented cats, wrapped in warm blankets, spooning.

The next morning, Clint and his new wife Wendy met us downstairs for breakfast. Their ranch was not far away.

"You look happier than a kid pulling a pup's ears," Clint said, slapping my back. Cassie blushed.

We filled up on homemade strawberry waffles hot off the griddle. After second helpings, Clint pushed back from the table and said, "Let's go burn off some calories and have some fun!"

With Clint and Wendy on one snowmobile and Cassie and me on the other, we chased each other up to a place called the bowl. Cassie squealed and held on to me tightly, clearly having a blast. We stopped and made a fire.

Cassie and I split off from Clint and Wendy and played in the snow, rolling over each other like a couple of frisky puppies. After a snowball fight, we fell back into the snow, panting.

She kissed me, spread out her knit hat in the snow, and made a snow pile on top of it, smiling impishly.

"You wouldn't!" I teased. Of course, she did, which started another round of snowball fighting. When we rejoined Clint and Wendy, Clint and I strapped on our skis and took turns pulling each other around with the snowmobile. We had not had this much fun together since junior high.

That night, the four of us had dinner at the lodge and danced to a live rock-and-roll band until midnight. They played all our old favorites from the sixties and seventies.

On the last song, the lead singer stepped up to the microphone and mumbled in a low, sexy voice, "This song is dedicated to Cassie, with love from Jeff." The crowd clapped; I stood up and held out my hand. Cassie blushed, and we stepped onto the dance floor all alone like lovesick teenagers. The band played the opening bars to "How Deep Is Your Love" by the Bee Gees, and the crowd swooned. We slow-danced under the spotlight and softly whispered the lyrics to each other as the band played on. I could not wait to get her back to the cabin.

On Sunday, we checked out, hoping to arrive at Clint and Wendy's ranch at Manastash Ridge as early as we could, so we could have time to ride horseback in the snow. While Wendy and Cassie were in the kitchen making sandwiches, Clint and I headed out to the barn to saddle up two retired Seattle police horses Clint had rescued.

"Cassie's good for you," Clint said. "It's great seeing you so happy."

"I was wondering what you thought of her," I said. "I think she's the one."

"Glad to hear it," Clint said, shaking my hand.

We saddled a couple of paints for the women. I had trouble with my horse as soon as we started on the trail. He had better things to do with his time, like stopping every few yards to nibble on whatever looked inviting. I had a hard time keeping up with the group. Wendy signaled Cassie and Clint to keep going while she waited for me to catch up.

"Let's exchange bridles; maybe that'll help," Wendy said. While she swapped bridles, she said, "You might want to keep Cassie around."

"Ya think?" I replied.

"Yep, she loves you," she said.

Two unsolicited thumbs up for Cassie from two of my closest friends topped off my weekend. I grinned all the way home. It was the best weekend of my life. I drove the long way home with the windows open, singing, "How Deep Is Your Love" at the top of my lungs.

When I got home, I noticed Cassie had left her little lingerie bag on the seat. I smiled when I thought about what was in the bag and replayed the memories of the weekend in my head. I picked up the bag to put it in a safe place in the truck, and a cassette fell out.

There was a note scrawled on the front of the cassette: "This song is for you. I love you more and more every day, Cassie."

I popped it in the cassette player. There was a single song on the tape entitled "If You Say My Eyes Are Beautiful" by Whitney Houston and Jermaine Jackson. I listened to it over and over again, memorizing the lyrics. It was as if the song had been specifically written for us. I carried the cassette inside and listened to it again on the stereo with the volume turned up. When I woke up the next morning, it was still playing.

Chapter 32

It was Christmas Eve morning. While Kyra was playing next door, Cassie pulled out the Christmas decorations that Abbey had carefully packed and stored. She hummed, "I Saw Mommy Kissing Santa Claus," as she decorated the tree.

"Is that tree big enough?" I asked. It was a tiny tree, small enough to sit on the coffee table with room to spare.

"Stop picking on the little tree," she said, winking at me.

"One big whack would turn it into a pile of toothpicks. We could hand them out after Christmas dinner."

"You're mean." She slapped the palm of her hand against my chest.

"Ow!"

"Poor, baby," she said, kissing the place she had slapped.

"Let's kiss and make up," I said.

We ripped off our clothes and made love on the floor next to the pile of bird ornaments, satin apples, red and silver tinsel, and the tangled strand of blinking lights.

Later that afternoon, I put on my best suit. Cassie slipped into her Sunday dress and dressed Kyra in white lace. We drove to the Bakers' for the annual Christmas gathering. I had become accustomed to the formal atmosphere, the elegant dinners and carefully worded conversation, though I was still more of an observer than a participant.

Christmas Day at Abbey's was more relaxed and fun. Abbey made matching blue pajamas with little black penguins for Stacey, Kyra, Gabe, and Jason. After dinner, the kids changed into their new pajamas and paraded around the living room, elbows linked together, waddling side to side in formation and squawking like penguins. Abbey took a picture, which turned out to be my favorite snapshot of the children together. It ended up framed and sitting on my desk at work.

I went alone to my token Christmas visit with Hazel. When I rolled up in front of her house, I had a firm plan: stay fifteen minutes tops. I grabbed some gifts from the back seat and joined the crowd. Hazel spotted me and hurried over.

After a minute or two of conversation, she asked, "How's the little monkey?"

"Shut up," I said, deeply offended by her remark.

"Get out," she said.

That was the last time I set foot in Hazel's house.

We celebrated New Year's Eve on Lake Union. Earlier in the day, I moved my boat from Lake Sammamish to Lake Union and tied it up at the Kayak Club. We invited all of our favorite people to join us for dinner. We stuffed ourselves silly, and after dinner, our party moved onto the boat. We pulled up anchor and found the perfect spot on the lake to watch the famous Lake Union New Year's Eve fireworks.

Just before midnight, while the others were distracted by the fireworks, I pulled Cassie into the cabin, where two silver-rimmed glasses filled with fresh strawberries soaked in Moet champagne sat on ice in a silver bucket surrounded by white roses. We fed each other strawberries and made New Year's resolutions. It was at midnight, while we were passionately kissing, that I silently made up my mind—1991 would be the year we would marry.

On a frigid morning in early February, I drove into Seattle. A thin layer of black ice covered the streets. I stopped at the red light on the corner of Fourth and Pike and assessed the downhill slope in front of me. I decided to go for it and eased downhill without sideswiping the cars parked on either side of the street. I turned into an open-air parking lot near Pike Place Market, walked down Pine Street, turned left on Post Alley, and stopped in front of a heavy metal door. I rang the bell.

The intercom above the bell came to life. "Good morning, state your name, please."

"I'm Jeffrey Green. I'm here for my 9:00 a.m. appointment."

The door opened, and I stepped inside. A heavyset, fully armed security guard led me upstairs, through several locked doors, and into a thickly carpeted chamber. A thin man with yellow-gray hair and thick eyebrows, dressed in a white shirt and black tie invited me into the vault. There were rows and rows of jewelry display cases.

"Where do you want to start, Mr. Green?" he said.

"I want to see the hearts."

"Pardon me, the hearts?"

"I mean the heart-shaped diamonds."

"Ah, yes, the hearts!" he said.

He shuffled through the display cases and placed a tray on the black-velvet countertop. I leaned over and scanned the diamonds. One stood out brighter than the rest in the middle of the bottom row.

"I'd like to see that one," I said.

He placed it in my hand. The shape was perfect, the color brilliant. The clerk stated the grade classification, the size of the carat, and went into detail about the location of the diamond's origin.

"I'll take it," I said.

"Do you know the ring size of the lucky recipient?"

I thought a while about this rather important question. I visualized Cassie's long, slender fingers and saw the ring glittering on her wedding finger. I saw her smiling with wet eyes.

"Size six," I said.

"If it needs to be resized later," he said, "we can do that." We talked about mountings, and he suggested a goldsmith nearby.

"The guard will escort the diamond to the goldsmith, Mr. Green. He will meet you there at the appointed time. Pardon me while I step out to give him a call," the sales clerk said.

A few minutes later, he returned and said, "It's all arranged."

On Valentine's Day, Cassie and I agreed to meet at Ruth's Chris Steakhouse at 7:00 p.m. I got there early and settled down in a comfortable chair, watching a large aquarium full of live lobsters clambering over each other.

The door opened, and Cassie walked into the lobby. She wore a red velvet dress. The velvet clung to her curves, and the V-shaped satin-rimmed neckline slightly exposed her freckled cleavage. Her dark hair fell in a mass of curls down her back and deepened against the red velvet. She walked across the room to the reservation desk, playing staccato notes on the hardwood floor with her six-inch black stiletto heels.

"Has Jeffrey Green arrived?"

I stepped to her side proudly. "Hello, gorgeous."

"Hi," she said, kissing me softly on the lips.

Several courses later, Cassie stepped away to freshen up a bit, and when she returned, the server was pouring a chilled bottle of French chardonnay. I ran over the rehearsed speech in my head, but at the last second, I tossed it out, reached across the table, and took her hands in mine.

"Cassie, will you marry me?"

She looked at me seriously. "Are you sure?"

"Yes."

"Me too," she said with misty eyes.

"So, you'll marry me?"

Tears ran down her face. She nodded.

We stood up. She put her arms around my neck and hugged me tightly. I thought of Kyra's famous hugs.

I gently opened her left hand, placed the ring in her palm, and closed her fingers around it.

She gasped. I slipped the ring on her finger. It fit. She stared at it, riling her wrist, watching it flicker in the candlelight.

"Oh, Jeff, it's perfect."

We lingered at the table awhile longer, looking deeply into each other's eyes. No words were necessary.

Cassie wanted to stop by her parents' house on the way home. When we got there, Frank and Rose were sitting in the den with Noah and Madelyn, watching the eleven o'clock news. Cassie walked to the television and stood in front of it.

"Look everybody!" she shouted, sticking her left hand straight out and wiggling her fingers.

Rose shouted, "Cassie, dear!" She rushed over and hugged her. After admiring the ring, Rose wrapped her arms around me and gave me a big smooch right on the lips.

Noah smiled. I smiled. Madelyn did not.

Frank chuckled and said, "Do you think you're poor now? Well, just wait, buddy boy!"

"Oh, Frank, shut up," Rose said endearingly.

Noah left the room to return shortly with a bottle of scotch and toasted to our happiness together. Madelyn was clearly displeased but said nothing.

When Cassie and I got home, she opened her purse and pulled out a small red envelope.

"I have a Valentine's gift for you too."

I opened the envelope, careful not to tear the flap. Inside was a white index card. A hand-drawn tiny red heart sat in the center; taped next to it, a small gold key. I looked at Cassie, puzzled.

"Turn it over," she said.

I flipped it over and read Cassie's handwriting.

To the man I love and trust with my life and the life of my daughter. The key to our hearts is yours. I will love you always, in this world and the next. Cassie.

I was so flooded with love that I did not know what to say. Cassie saw the tears in my eyes and understood.

The next morning, when Cassie told Kyra about our plans, she was one happy little girl. She talked nonstop about her new daddy. When I picked her up from school, she was standing on the curb, waiting for me, along with a group of her girlfriends.

"That's my new daddy," she said to her friends, who stared at me silently as she hopped in and hugged my neck tightly.

Immediately after we announced our engagement, Cassie began obsessing about the wedding. Bridal magazines piled up on the coffee table at her place. Her personal date book overflowed with cut-out pictures of wedding dresses, flower arrangements, silver, and china patterns. She was on the phone constantly consulting Abbey or Meredith about the wedding protocols.

We told the boys together, who were thrilled with the idea of having two mommies who loved them and a brand-new sister.

Cassie wanted to be married in the Catholic church, so I agreed to attend classes on Catholicism. It would take time to satisfy the criteria requested by the local diocese, at least six months or more. We also felt it would be appropriate to give the kids time to adjust to becoming part of a new family. A definitive wedding date would take some time to pinpoint, but I was okay with that. I wanted everything to be proper and perfect for Cassie.

Near the end of February, I found a note in my truck.

Jeff, meet me at 6:30 p.m. at the Lake Bellevue Café. Dad will watch Kyra for us tonight. I love you, C.

I panicked for a minute, remembering the last time Cassie summoned me to meet her, spilling the beans about her past. I read the note again, realizing the tone was upbeat, and laughed at myself for thinking the worst.

It was a busy day, with a project deadline coming up, but I was able to show up on time at the café. The waiter led me to a dimly lit room in the back. Cassie met me at the door with a kiss. Suddenly, the room lit up.

"Surprise!"

With all the excitement of the past few weeks, I had forgotten that it was my birthday. Our friends, Cassie's brother, and all the people from work were there.

The servers brought in a multilayered white cake with caramel icing. There was one huge candle in the center instead of thirty-six little ones. I was not the kind of person to be easily surprised, but for the first time in my life, I was flabbergasted.

Cassie gave me a black leather bomber jacket. In time, the jacket would become my second skin, and I would wear it until it fell apart.

In the middle of March, on St. Patrick's Day, Gabe and Jason had their first sleepover at the condominium with Cassie, Kyra, and me. It was rehearsal weekend for our new family. We celebrated St. Patrick's Day with green sherbet and Kool-Aid for the kids and green beer for Cassie and me. The kids colored and cut out shamrocks and taped them to the kitchen windows.

On Sunday evening, Cassie and Kyra drove back to their apartment, and I drove the boys back to Jen's house. When I got home, the phone was ringing.

"I'm scared," Cassie said, her voice trembling. "Will you come over?"

"I'm scared too, Daddy. Please hurry," Kyra whimpered in the background.

"I'm on my way."

I found Cassie standing in the living room, pointing to the ceiling. Kyra jumped into my arms and buried her face in my chest. There was a bullet hole in the ceiling directly above where Cassie was standing.

"Wait here," I said. I ran upstairs and knocked on the door. A frightened man in his early twenties opened the door and let me in. He said he was a rookie cop and that he was cleaning his gun and thought it was empty when it went off. He had been on the job for two weeks.

I called the Bellevue Police Department, reported the incident, and actually felt a little sorry for him when the officer showed up and took his gun away.

"Don't leave, Daddy," Kyra said when I returned. "I'm still scared."

"I won't leave, honey. I'm right here."

I sat next to her bedside and held her until she fell asleep. When I woke up the next morning, stiff from sleeping in the chair, Cassie was standing in the doorway, smiling.

"You must have a sore back," she said.

I stood up and stretched.

"Why don't you take a shower, and I'll make coffee," Cassie said.

"The shower part sounds good," I said.

Cassie made the worst coffee. No amount of sugar or cream helped. Fortunately, the pot of coffee never materialized.

When I was in the shower, Cassie let her robe slip to the floor and stepped in with me. Showering with a woman was something I had fantasized about but had never experienced. It was a long, hot, steamy shower. Cassie knew exactly what to do with her lathered hands. It was wonderful. In the middle of the shower, I thought I heard the door open. I peeked out, but no one was there.

I was late to work that morning, and once there, I found it difficult to focus on anything but our morning shower.

Cassie and Kyra picked me up after work and took me to dinner. After sitting down at the table, Kyra put her hand over her mouth and giggled.

"Go ahead," Cassie said to Kyra.

She sat straight up and gave me her best smile. "Daddy?"

"Yes, Kyra?"

"Will you be my dad, my for-real dad?"

I had no idea how to answer that question. If I had said yes and it ended up that I could not legally adopt her, then I would betray her by telling her yes. If I said no, she would think that I did not want to be her dad. I smiled and let the moment pass. I had no way of knowing that soon I would bitterly regret not saying yes when I had the chance.

In the days that followed, Cassie and I talked about buying a house. Cassie found a house in Clyde Hill, an upscale neighborhood east of Seattle. The two-level house was approximately three thousand square feet, with four bedrooms, three baths, and a nice backyard with a sweeping view of the Seattle skyline from the second-floor deck. She fell in love with it.

The house I liked was in Bridle Trails in Kirkland, a nice neighborhood but not as upscale as Clyde Hill. It was the same square footage as the first house, but it was a single-level, ranch-style house with lots of floor-to-ceiling windows overlooking a huge backyard with mature fruit trees and a garden. We agreed to disagree and continued to search for a house that we both loved equally.

On the morning of March 27, after sleeping over at Cassie's apartment, I woke up an hour early to help Kyra with a school project. After I dropped her off at school, I drove back to the apartment to pick up my briefcase. I knocked on the door, but Cassie had already left for work. I unlocked the door with my set of keys, grabbed my briefcase, and noticed a message on the answering machine. Before thinking it through, I pressed the play button.

"Hey, baby, it's Charlie."

If I could have reached through the other end of that machine and strangled the bastard with his own phone cord, I would have.

"How's our daughter?" the message continued. "I think about her a lot. You know what I mean? Her birthday is coming up soon. She's about to be five years old, and I have not seen her since she was only a day old. It isn't right, Cassie. I need to see her. I'm coming to Seattle this Friday, and I want to spend time with her. You owe me that much. My flight arrives at 3:25 p.m., Alaska Airlines, flight 750. Meet me at the gate with my girl. Tell her Daddy is coming to town."

I wanted to rip the answering machine out of the wall. Instead, I erased the message. The last thing Kyra needed was to meet that weasel of a father, especially now that she wanted me to be her dad.

On Friday, a little before three, I showed up at gate 13D at SeaTac. I was early, and the plane had not landed yet.

"Don't get up on account of me," Clint said, extending his hand.

"I'm glad you could come. I needed backup," I said.

"No problem, Jeff. Happy to help, you know that."

A few minutes later, Mitchell and Aaron walked up and sat down beside us.

"Good, we're all here," I said.

"I checked arrivals. Flight 750 just touched down," Aaron said.

I turned to Mitchell. "Are you sure you know what he looks like?" I asked.

"I'm pretty sure. Cassie showed me his picture right after she was released from rehab."

The flight attendant opened the door to the gate and secured it. The four of us moved toward the front of the crowd of onlookers. One by one, well-dressed first-class passengers in business attire trickled into the waiting area and out into the terminal corridor.

I looked at Mitchell. He shook his head; no, not yet. A large group of passengers crammed through the doorway. I watched Mitchell scan the crowd. Then he stopped and fixed his glasses. I wheeled around, ready to get a good look at the man who nearly destroyed Cassie's life.

"That's him," Mitchell said pointing at a tall, rail-thin black man with a heavily acne-scarred face and long dreadlocked hair. He wore blue, gray, and silver sweats and a matching jacket. On his right index finger was a large gold ring with some sort of engraved insignia.

"Let's take the bastard somewhere and leave him," Clint said.

"Don't get crazy, Clint. We're sticking to the plan," Mitchell said.

"I've never been that fond of suntans," Clint said, snickering and elbowing me.

"Code four," I said, which in Jeff/Clint language meant *shut the fuck up.*

Mitchell approached him. "Are you Charlie Mullins?" he asked.

"Who wants to know?" he replied. His voice sounded hoarse and scratchy.

Clint blurted out, "There's a flight leaving for Anchorage in forty-five minutes." Clint had a six-pack abdomen and legendary left hook to back up his words. He was not someone you could ignore easily.

Charlie looked at him and said, "Why? Are you going to Anchorage?"

"No, you are," Clint said.

"Look, I'm not here to make trouble. I'm here to see my daughter," he said.

The words *my daughter* hit me deep in my gut.

"Well, I don't know about *your* daughter, but *my* daughter is staying at my house this weekend," I said. I made a fist, ready to jump him.

"Who are you?" Charlie said.

"I'm the only father Kyra knows," I said. "And it's going to stay that way."

"There are black men and then there are n-----," Clint said, moving close to Charlie's face. "A black man would be smart enough to get back on the airplane; a n----- would be stupid enough to stay."

"Is there a problem here?" an airport security guard interrupted, stepping in between Charlie and Clint.

Mitchell said, "No, officer, we're just waiting here for our friend to catch a flight."

The officer backed off a few steps but continued to monitor us.

Charlie eyed the four of us. We engaged him in a stare-down. Clearly outnumbered, Charlie backed down.

Mitchell, Aaron, Clint, and I surrounded him and walked him down to the baggage claim area. He picked up his bags, Aaron handed him the ticket back to Anchorage, and we escorted him to the departure gate. It was as quick as that. Charlie left Seattle without any of us ever telling him our names.

That evening, when Cassie was on the phone with Abbey, discussing more wedding details, Kyra and I played a game of Candy Land.

Kyra made a funny face and said, "Daddy, what were you and Mommy doing in the shower?"

What a kid moment that was! "Well, Kyra, you know I love your mommy, right?"

"Sure, Daddy, and she loves you too."

"Well, see, sometimes adults do things with each other when they love each other. It is very, very private, just between adults and not for kids. Understand?" I said.

I was relieved that she seemed satisfied with my answer.

A few days later, Cassie, Kyra, Gabe, Jason, and I boarded a plane for Disneyland. We celebrated all three kids' birthdays with a big party, attended by Mickey Mouse, Cinderella, and Snow White. The boys loved their Goofy hats, and Kyra went wild over the magic wand that Cinderella's fairy godmother gave her.

The warm weather made us giddy, especially after the long, harsh winter. We spent a lot of time sunning by the pool. A week later, we flew home, slightly sunburned and closer than ever.

Chapter 33

On Monday, April 16, the day after Easter, Cassie, Kyra and I started the day with a quick breakfast together. We talked about the busy day ahead.

"Don't forget, Jeff, Kyra has a dentist appointment this afternoon at three thirty," Cassie said as she grabbed her purse and fumbled for her car keys.

"No problem. I'll take care of it," I said.

"Gotta go," Cassie said as she blew kisses at Kyra and me.

I made a note of the dentist appointment and then drove Kyra to school. Sticking out of her backpack was Kyra's new pink wand from Disneyland.

"You're taking your wand to school again today?" I asked.

"Sure, it's magic, you know," she said very seriously.

She sang "It's a Small World" the rest of the way to school. At the drop-off point, Kyra held on to our hug a little longer than usual.

"I love you, Daddy," she said. She put her little hands on my face and steadied herself while she kissed my cheek and then turned my face and kissed the other cheek. Kyra could warm my heart on the coldest day of winter.

"I love you too, Kyra. Have a good day. See you this afternoon."

She skipped down the sidewalk and joined her friends. It was a sunny, mild spring day. The cherry blossoms along the mountainsides were at their peak.

I stopped by the post office to mail a few bills. There was a long line of cars, and the parking lot was full too. April 15 fell on Easter Sunday that year, so the tax deadline was officially the day after. Having already mailed my taxes, I was not willing to wait in line for long. The post office could wait another day.

When I got to the office, I glanced at my schedule and saw a conflict in the afternoon that would interfere with me picking up Kyra. I called Cassie.

"I'm sorry, Cassie. Do you mind picking up Kyra today? I completely forgot about the boat show. I just noticed it on my calendar. I have my heart set on this on antique wooden boat, a real beauty. Mind if I beg off?"

"Of course I don't mind. Have fun at the show. I'll pick Kyra up and take her to the dentist appointment."

We made plans to meet for dinner out at six. "See you this evening," I told her.

"Jeff?"

"Yes?"

"I love you," she said.

"I like the sound of that. I love you too. Save a kiss for me. See you at dinner." I hung up.

In Bellevue that same afternoon at 3:10, Burt was driving on Northeast Eighth in his Digger Derrick truck he lovingly named Bluebell. Traffic was bumper-to-bumper but not stalled. Burt turned on the radio and tuned in to KOMO 1000 on the AM band to listen to the traffic report at a quarter after the hour. The wife would be pleased to see him home early. He turned the volume up so he could hear over the noise of Bluebell's engine. He thought he might do a little yard work when he got the home. The traffic ahead gained some momentum. He coasted through the green light at 116th Avenue Northeast and shifted gears as he prepared to drive over the I-405 bridge, take the Cloverleaf exit, and merge into heavy traffic heading south on I-405 to Renton. In front of him was a woman in a dull-green Hyundai. Burt saw her smiling and chatting with the little girl strapped in the back seat.

The glare from the western sun lit up in the dirt and grime on the windshield, temporarily obscuring Burt's view ahead. He opened the glove compartment and fumbled for his sunglasses, slipping them on with one hand while guiding Bluebell with the other as he drove over the bridge. As his vision cleared, he noticed some commotion at the traffic lights and the sound of screeching brakes spread like wildfire straight toward him.

Burt rammed his foot hard on the brake. He felt gravity's heavy hand pushing Bluebell forward. He screamed when the truck hit something hard, lifting him out of his seat, snapping his head back. He lost his sense of direction. Like falling dominoes, he heard wham after wham as cars crashed into each other. Then all was still.

His sunglasses were gone. He tried to focus, but what he saw was a revolving world of powder-blue sky, red streaks of light, white glare, and the drab grays of the pavement. He closed his eyes to stop the dizzy feeling. There was a painful pressure on the left side of his body. He was dangling sideways, still strapped in his seat. He opened his eyes again. The merry-go-round of colored lights had stopped. He looked to his left and saw pavement. Debris cluttered the street. He could make out a spiral-bound notebook lying open, its white pages flipping in the breeze, reflecting the sun's glare. He moved his head to the right and saw clear blue sky out the passenger's side window.

The truck came to rest on its side, driver's side down. It had fallen on something; he shuddered to think what it was.

With some maneuvering, he could release the door and let it fall open under its own weight. He stepped on the steering wheel, braced his legs, and unbuckled the seat belt. His right hand grabbed the steering wheel, and he slowly lowered his body far enough down to grasp the door handle. The door quickly fell open and hit the pavement. He slid his body out of the cab and landed on the road, facing the mangled wreckage underneath.

Something caught his eye, lying on the pavement near the rear of the wreckage. It looked like a child's toy, maybe a baton or some kind of wand. It had broken open and was oozing a sticky-looking mixture of glitter and blood. Burt willed his arms and legs to move. He slowly got up on all fours and crawled away from the truck. A soft, faint voice called out. He crawled back under the truck.

"Mommy ..." the little girl whispered, faintly moaning.

"Hold on, honey," Burt said. "Help is coming."

He backed away from the wreckage and crawled out from under the truck. A firefighter covered him with a blanket. Two more firefighters bent down and looked under the truck, talking softly to each other.

Burt walked unsteadily to the right side of the truck. Attached to Bluebell's front fender and bent up like an accordion was the roof of the green Hyundai.

Lying face up on the street, wedged against the concrete railing, overlooking I-405 was a young, dark-haired woman, her body crumpled as if it were a pile of litter tossed to the side of the road. Blood soaked her long, black hair and her clothes and trickled down the street toward Burt. Ambulance personnel rushed past Burt toward the woman.

Dizziness overtook him again. He began to fall.

"Hold on there, buddy," a man said, catching him.

"Save the little girl, not me," Burt said, bursting into tears.

The man placed him face up on a stretcher, rolled him over on his right side, and attached EKG leads. He caught a glimpse of the firefighters still working to get the girl out.

A group of men placed Burt into an ambulance nearby. Someone covered his face with an oxygen mask. Burt attempted to raise his head up enough to peer out the rear windows of the ambulance as it pulled onto 116th Avenue Northeast and sped toward Overlake Medical Center emergency room a half mile away. A sharp, stabbing pain pierced the base of his neck and radiated down his spine. The technician pulled the window shades down and shut out the white sunlight.

Chapter 34

Boat lovers like me packed the convention center. I was just beginning to negotiate with the dealer of the antique boat I wanted when the loudspeaker interrupted our conversation. "Jeffrey Green, come to the information desk immediately."

"Excuse me, that's me," I said to the dealer. "I'll be right back." I elbowed through the crowd to the information desk. A middle-aged man wearing a ship captain's hat asked, "Can I help you?"

"I'm Jeff Green. Do you have a message for me?"

"Oh, yes, a Mr. Noah Baker called. He said to tell you that it's urgent." The man wrote a number down and handed it to me.

"May I use your phone?" I asked.

"Sure," he said. He picked up the phone behind the counter and pushed it over toward me. "Dial 9 to get an outside line."

"Thanks." I said as I began to dial the numbers.

"Noah, this is Jeff. Is there something wrong?"

"Jeff ..."

"What is it?"

"Cassie and Kyra have been in a car accident."

"Where are they?"

"At Overlake; we're here in the waiting room."

"I'm on my way."

"Hurry. It's serious."

I could not get to Overlake fast enough. I pulled into the breezeway outside the emergency room and walked through the sliding glass doors into the waiting area. Noah, Madelyn, Aaron, Mitchell, Scott, and Meredith were there.

"Where are they?" I asked.

"Walk with me," Scott said.

"Not now. I need to stay here in case we get some news."

Scott and I stepped outside. As we walked down the sidewalk, Scott slowed down and stopped. He turned to face me.

"This is what I know. Cassie and Kyra were on the on-ramp. Traffic backed up I-405 and Northeast Eighth. There was a wreck ahead, and Cassie slammed on the brakes to avoid crashing into the car in front of her. A Derrick truck, the kind that puts telephone poles in the ground, went right over the top of Cassie's car. Kyra was in the back seat. It was a multivehicle pileup."

I ran as fast as I could back to the emergency room with Scott running just behind me. People from Cassie's workplace were now in the waiting room. A female physician with a thick Irish accent and red hair stood beside Noah and Madelyn, talking to them in low tones. I broke through the crowd, approached the doctor, and overheard her say, "Only one family member can go in."

Madelyn stepped up. Noah put his hand on her shoulder and pushed her back out of the way. Mitchell gave me a push. Noah nodded.

I followed the doctor through locked doors and down a corridor of treatment rooms shielded by white cotton curtains, some open, some closed. I thought I heard a child crying. I stopped, listened again. An old man began coughing violently. I moved on.

The doctor stopped in from of the treatment room at the end of the hall. The curtains were drawn shut. "You can see her now," she said.

She opened the door, and I stepped inside the room. The first thing I noticed was the silence. No monitors were beeping, no lights blinking, and the switch on the oxygen panel embedded in the wall was in the off position.

Cassie lay in the bed, her eyes closed. Her hair was tangled and gooey with blood. Her face was clean and very pale. White sheets covered the rest of her body, even her arms and her hands. There were no tubes in her mouth or nose. She looked like she was sleeping. I waited for her to wake up and look at me, to see that I was there beside her.

I moved a little closer. Her chest was still. There was no sign of respiration. I kissed her. Her lips were cold and hard.

"Cassie, come back."

I waited in the silence for a long time.

"Jeff, it's late. Let us take you home," Meredith said, Scott standing beside her.

I sat in the back seat of Scott's patrol car, shaking uncontrollably. I grabbed the seat to try to steady myself. Meredith and Scott were talking to me, but I could not understand what they were saying. I was in some kind of limbo, as if I had one foot planted wherever Cassie was and the other foot in the car with them.

At the condominium, Meredith and Scott sat with me on the couch.

"It should have been me. I was supposed to take Kyra to the dentist," I said.

"It's not your fault, Jeff," Scott said. "It was an accident. Blaming yourself won't bring her back."

I did blame myself. What I had done was unforgivable. Meredith moved closer to me and took my hand. Her cold hands trembled. I searched her face.

"Kyra passed away at 5:35 p.m., while you were in with Cassie."

The crying began. I broke down. When I regained my composure, I said, "Thank you both for bringing me home. If you don't mind, I'd like to be alone now."

After they left, I went into Kyra's bedroom and sat on her bed. "Kyra, I know you are here. I can feel you in this room with me. I heard you calling for me in the emergency room. I heard you, but I went to see your mom instead." I broke down again.

"I'm sorry I wasn't there," I sobbed. "Please forgive me."

The crying lasted for hours. I fell back on Kyra's bed. The stillness came back. I called for Kyra again. I saw her round, dark eyes and dimpled smile. I heard her running down the hall, giggling. She was wearing her blue penguin pajamas.

The next day, I went to the wrecking yard to see what was left of the Hyundai. It was no taller than a kitchen table and completely unrecognizable.

Cassie's funeral took place at the Catholic church in Bellevue, the one she had attended since she was a child. Family and friends of the Bakers attended. None of my family showed up, and I preferred it that way.

I sat in the pew behind the Baker family; Abbey was with me. When the music started, all the pews had filled up. I cried when the pallbearers carried the brilliant white, rose-covered caskets down the aisle, one small and one large.

After the funeral, Mitchell invited Abbey and me to come to the Baker house. I rang the doorbell, and Madelyn opened the door. She was still wearing her black suit from the funeral. Her small, gray eyes were surprisingly soft and kind as she looked at me. She took my right hand and held it with both of her hands. Her fingers wrapped around mine, embracing them. She did not speak. The moment of warmth was over quickly.

The house was so full of people that I felt suffocated. I stepped out the back door to get some fresh air, walked out to the tennis courts, and sat down in a lawn chair. I would not go back inside and would never set foot in that house again. After a while, Abbey came outside to join me.

"It's a zoo in there," she said. "Let's get out of here."

"Take my truck home," I said, throwing her my keys. "I want to sit here awhile longer."

"Are you sure?" Abbey said. "Do you want me to come back and get you?"

"No, no. I'll get home somehow," I told her. "I'll call you if I need you."

Fog covered the valley below the grounds; only the tips of conifers were visible. Mitchell and Aaron walked toward me, carrying folding chairs. They sat down on either side of me. We sat in the quiet and waited for the fog to roll in.

Eventually, Mitchell said, "Hey, Aaron, remember the time we put Cassie's bra in the freezer?"

"Sure do," Aaron chuckled. "Remember what she did to get back at us?"

"How could I forget?" he said with a smile. One story after another followed, as Mitchell and Aaron reminisced about happier times when they were growing up with Cassie.

"I think I'll go for a walk," I said, shaking their hands and thanking them. I walked down the street and disappeared into the fog. My heart ached for Cassie and Kyra. I walked for a long time, crying intermittently, and ended up at a neighborhood convenience store. I called a cab and went home to the empty condominium.

Not long after the funeral, I left town. I could not stand sleeping another night in the condo. Abbey agreed to see to it while I was gone and worked on finding a new place for me in my absence. Clint and Wendy had some friends who owned a hunting camp in Alaska. They asked me to come for a visit after they heard about what happened.

Clint's friend Joe took me out to an island off the coast of Alaska in his fishing boat and left me there. I slept in a tent and camped with meager supplies. I was there for a month. I let nature take a crack at healing me. The harsh climate felt good.

I went back home on Memorial Day 1991. Abbey had been successful in finding a house for me. I stopped by the condominium for the last time and opened the front door. It was empty except for a few boxes left behind that Abbey did not know what to do with. I walked in and out of the empty rooms, opened the closet doors, and checked the bathroom for anything Abbey may have missed in the move. I grabbed the keys to the new house. On the way, out I noticed a small UPS package on my counter. It was from Noah and Madelyn Baker.

I picked up the package and went down to the dock to my boat. The motor started right away. I drove out into the middle of the lake, stopped the motor, and drifted.

The package lay on the seat next to me. I opened it. Inside were two things: a small sealed envelope and a diary. I opened the envelope. The crystal bear necklace that I gave Kyra on that first Christmas Eve slipped out of the envelope and fell into my hand. On the surface of the water, I saw Kyra standing in front of the Christmas tree, wearing the necklace, smiling and showing her dimples. Cassie knelt beside her. The necklace slipped between my fingers, almost dropping into the water. Catching the necklace became the most important thing.

I slipped the necklace and locked diary in my jacket pocket, parked the boat, and drove to the new house. It was a small one-story house with light-gray exterior siding and a small but sufficient backyard. I unlocked the sliding glass door and walked into the house. The sofa and chairs were light-blue canvas. Posters of Washington beaches hung on the walls. A basket of seashells sat on the dining room table. I liked it. I thought I could live there.

I sat in one of the chairs and pulled out the diary again. The cover was pink leather. I touched the worn slick spots near the lock and turned the diary over in my hand several times until the leather felt warm. This had to be Cassie's diary. But where was the key?

I remembered the key Cassie had given me on Valentine's Day. I went to the bedroom and looked for a box labeled "Jeff's personal things." I opened it and found the small white card with the little heart in the center. I unfastened the key and slipped it into the lock. The latch fell open.

I read throughout the afternoon and into the night. I fell in love with her all over again, even after reading about the things she kept hidden. It was as if Cassie had come back to pay me one last visit.

I turned to the day we first met: November 4, 1989.

I met a man at the park with gorgeous blue eyes and a kind face.

I turned to the last entry eighteen months later, April 16, 1991.

Abbey went with me to buy my wedding dress this morning. I love the tiny pearls around the waist and on the sleeves. I hope Jeff loves it as much as I do. And Kyra's dress! Oh, my! She will look like an angel on our wedding day! I can't wait to see Jeff's face when he sees her in it.

Note to self: Don't forget to pick up both dresses from the seamstress this weekend.

There were several blank lines and then a hastily scribbled note.

I'm writing this at work on my lunch hour, so I need to go, since I'm leaving early today. Last night, Jeff was incredible. Lying in his arms, listening to his steady breathing, I felt safe and warm and loved completely. I am at peace with myself at last. Sometimes I wonder what a child of ours would look like. Jeff would freak out if he knew I was thinking of having a child with him. *I promised not to keep secrets, but he doesn't have to know about this, at least not yet.*

I closed the diary, locked it, and put it away for safekeeping.

I picked up the phone and called a familiar number. Gabe answered.

"Hey, buddy, I'm home," I said.

"Daddy!" he said.

"You and your brother get your gear ready. We're going fishing!"

Printed in the United States
by Baker & Taylor Publisher Services